Vile Blood 3
REUNION

Published by Jen Golembiewski

http://jengolembiewski.weebly.com/

Follow me on Twitter: @JenGolembiewski

Like my Facebook Page:
http://www.facebook.com/vilebloodseries

Rate/Review this book at:
https://www.goodreads.com/book/show/30122028-
reunion

Dedication

For Tony; my rock, my best friend, and the love of my life.

Prologue

Light came from every angle, its warmth turned searing. Golden embers sparked and burned at her flesh. The odor was pungent; the stench coming from her bubbling skin. The heat overcame her and gave her no relief; she could not die and the pain would not stop. The flames kept coming at her, they would not dissipate. She was the wick of the candle, and surrounded by fuel. Caged in hell with an eternity to atone, the burning would last forever, and she prayed to be ash.

Only love would set her free.

Chapter 1

Seven years had passed since Sarain first learned of her true origins, and in that time she learned to cope with the changes within her body, but has never truly accepted it. She spent her time in hiding, more closed off than ever, sticking to the shadows like a creature, hoping to keep off her father's radar. She trained and honed her skills, and learned how to properly use her growing power. Sarain continued to hunt demons, picking them off like cattle, and never staying in one area too long.

Sarain studied and researched everything she could possibly find on demon folklore, anything that could teach her what her father was and how to kill him, but nothing panned out, and any shred of credibility in what she found all pointed to the same results: sunlight, fire, holy emblems, dismemberment, and destroying the heart. All which killed ordinary demons, but Aion wasn't ordinary. Sarain already knew that holy emblems and sunlight had no effect on him, and she wasn't sure if the rest would either. Besides, Aion was far quicker and stronger than Sarain. Even with all her training, she doubted she was strong enough yet to take him on, and she wasn't sure if she'd ever be.

All Sarain could hope for was that by tracking Aion's moves perhaps she could find something to use against him. She looked into places he had been to, and accounts that sounded like his work. She dragged herself home, one night, after a short trip out of town, looking into a possible "Ancient" account, but nothing viable could be found. The best Sarain got from the trip was a tip from another hunter claiming that an "Ancient" had been reported recently in a nearby town called Shaven, and that the town itself was apparently strange as well. He said he had already checked the tip out himself, and found no evidence to back it, and that the town seemed ordinary. But he told Sarain that she could check for herself if she was so inclined. With nothing else to go on, this town was Sarain's only choice. She just needed to collect her things first before traveling there.

She carried a small backpack on her back as she trekked to her dwelling, the moon lighting her way. Her place wasn't in the best part of town, and she wondered if her lack of being around would have gotten her place broken into. She knew it was safe from demons; well, demons that weren't Aion, because she had set up a barrier around it, but that barrier did not keep out bad humans.

As her dwelling came into sight, the place looked untouched; the door was shut and the windows intact. Sarain felt a sigh of relief, and she approached her door. She started up the steps leading to it, but then suddenly stopped; she felt strange. Sarain began to feel sick like her energy was being drained. She quickly reached for her door knob, to go inside, when sparks immediately burnt at Sarain's fingers. She moved her hand back in pain and then reached with her other hand, and the same thing happened. Sarain took a step back and looked at her door. Everything appeared normal, she heard no sound of electrical frequency that could be causing the sparks, and then it hit Sarain. Her barrier, the one she set up herself to protect her place from demons, and that she had been living with for weeks, was suddenly keeping her out.

Sarain felt no different from when she had left her place days ago, but something must have changed. She stared at her door for a long moment, recalling all that was inside; weapons, clothes, food, but nothing precious. Sarain then turned around and walked down her steps. She would be heading to Shaven sooner than expected.

Sarain sat staring across the table, enamored with her dinner guest. Orran gazed back with his hazel eyes and a slight smile on his face; a half smirk he always made when talking to Sarain. Candles burned at the center of the table, dimly lighting the room. Their plates were empty and the dishes were sparklingly clean. Half full wine glasses stood untouched as the pair only saw one another.

Orran gently caressed Sarain's hand with his from across the table while staring at her lovingly. She felt herself blush like a young school girl in the presence of her crush. Orran smiled at Sarain's fluster, and told her, "You are so cute when you're embarrassed." She got redder.

Sarain had wanted to say so much to Orran. She worked up the courage to tell him, "I've been waiting for you…for a long time now." His face suddenly turned serious, and he let go of Sarain's hand and got up from his chair. He walked over slowly to her, and leaned down. Sarain looked up at Orran as he moved in, and she heard him whisper, "You can stop waiting." She closed her eyes and waited for him to kiss her, but the kiss never came.

Sarain suddenly remembered that none of this had ever happened; she was dreaming.

Sarain opened her eyes as her bus pulled into the small station. She looked around to see that not that many people were on her bus; Shaven was a small town that lacked visitors. She got up after the bus came to a full stop and the driver opened the doors. She grabbed her one backpack and headed off the bus. Sarain stepped down into the cool night air and looked up at the bright moon and the starry sky; it was a beautiful night.

Sarain glanced around the station, and spotted a janitor emptying the garbage cans. She approached the man and asked him, "Excuse me, but do you know anywhere I can find a place to stay for the night?" The janitor gazed at Sarain with puzzlement, and then replied, "You came here with no one to visit?" She looked confused and answered, "Yes, actually that's true…" The janitor then quickly said, "Sorry about that, we don't get many tourists here in Shaven unless they're visiting a local… Umm, let me think… There's the Scarlet Motel.

It's not too far from here, just down that street over there, you can't miss it; it has a big neon red sign."

"Okay, thanks," Sarain replied. She then turned and headed down the road she was shown. As she walked, she noticed how out of time the town was; she saw few cars, small plain looking homes all with old fashioned looking structures. The roads were laid with gravel, there were no sidewalks, and the street signs were all wooden. When Sarain finally reached the Scarlet Motel, it stood out as the only modern building around with its flashy neon sign, but even it looked a bit rundown.

Sarain went inside, and walked to the check in desk. There a scruffy man slept in his chair, snoring loudly. Sarain rang the service bell three times before he woke, and when he did, he stared at her stupefied for a second before finally saying, "I haven't seen you here before." Sarain looked at the man with annoyance and said, "No, that's why I'm checking in." The man stared at her for a moment longer as if trying to decipher something, it made Sarain uncomfortable, and then he asked, "Are you staying by the hour or by the day?"

Sarain realized what it was the man had been thinking, he was wondering if she was a prostitute. She immediately answered, "By the day," in a firm voice. The man handed Sarain a log book to sign in, as he muttered, "We don't get many overnighters." It was a comment that Sarain could have done without, because it told her more about the kind of place the motel was then she had wanted to know. Though on the plus side the man didn't ask her many questions, and allowed her to pay in cash. She signed in with a fake name, as she believed the other attendants before her had done. He then handed her a key, and Sarain went on her way.

Sarain found the room easily; it was the last one at the very end of the motel. She went to open the door and the knob stuck for a moment, but she forced the door open. She turned on the light, and immediately found the room detestable; the carpet was worn and dirty, the sheets were stained, the room was poorly lit, there was a large mirror above the bed, and everything was a dingy shade of red.

She groaned with disgust as she stepped in and closed the door behind her. She placed her bag on the bed, and feared seeing the bathroom. Regardless, Sarain cleaned herself up from her long bus ride, and changed into her only other set of clothes; another all black outfit that mostly covered her from neck to toe. She let down her long, wavy, black hair and it fell to her waist.

Sarain then went to the door, and stepped outside. She walked back to the motel's office where the scruffy guy sat bored. He looked up as she stepped inside, her hair seemed to catch his attention, and now he stared at Sarain even more than he did before.

"Is your room alright?" he asked her curiously. "Its fine," she muttered in reply, then asked, "Is there anywhere in town I can buy some supplies? Clothes and such." The man thought for a moment, and then answered, "We don't have many stores, and most of them would be closed by now… You can try the marketplace though, it's always active."

The idea of a marketplace seemed very old fashioned to Sarain, but she asked anyway, "Where is it?" "On the outskirts of town," the man replied, and then he added, "But not everyone there takes kindly to strangers; it's not really a place for tourists." "I think I'll be fine," Sarain responded. The man shrugged and said, "Suit yourself."

Sarain left and set out to find this market place. She still had a few hours until dawn and felt like exploring the town. The streets were dark with only a few streetlamps to light the way, but Sarain did not have trouble seeing; her night vision had developed quite well over the years. Sarain walked quickly, looking down each road to learn what she could about the area as she headed toward this marketplace. She trekked weaponless, having left all her weapons back in her last dwelling, unable to retrieve them, but she didn't worry much about it. She still felt plenty able to defend herself.

The walk went by fast, the town wasn't very big, but Sarain had trouble locating the marketplace. She looked around, but didn't see it in the street where the man described. Then she noticed light coming from a narrow opening between two buildings. Sarain walked towards the light and realized that it led to a nearly hidden alleyway full of vendors. The alley opened up wider than Sarain expected and she wondered how this was possible without seriously limiting the space of the buildings around it; it was like the dimensions didn't fit.

Candles lit up the marketplace making it almost look romantic. The vendors decorated their booths with colorful cloths and designs, and more people walked the area than Sarain had anticipated. She made her way slowly through the alleyway, looking at what the booths had to offer. Sarain noticed she was catching many stares, and it was obvious to everyone that she was an outsider. A few people didn't seem to mind her, but others gave her dirty or curious looks. The women more so than the men, seemed displeased with Sarain as though she were some kind of harlot, and a few men did indeed stare at Sarain as though she were a grand prize.

Sarain tried to avoid eye contact as she walked through the alley, not just to hide her unique eyes, but out of discomfort. Then she suddenly found herself unable to avoid one particular set of eyes; a pair of vibrant blue eyes that gazed at Sarain with amazement and disbelief. Sarain's breath caught in her throat as she instantly recognized her spectator. She stood still and stiff as she stared blankly forward, not sure of what to do.

Really, what could she say to Winston?

Chapter 2

Sarain stared at Winston for a while, as he did her. His blond hair was longer than the last time she had seen him, but everything else about him looked the same. Except he wasn't alone; on his arm was a young woman with fair skin and blond hair. The woman looked confused by Winston's sudden reaction, but soon realized that he was staring at Sarain. After another hesitant moment went by, Winston finally walked towards Sarain, his companion in tow.

Sarain took a deep breath to prepare herself for what was about to happen as Winston approached her. He stopped clearly in front of Sarain, his face expressionless, and he asked in an emotionless tone, "What are you doing here?" She quickly replied, "I'm on business," and then after a moment of silence, she added, "I didn't know you'd be here."

Winston gazed at Sarain for a moment while searching his thoughts, and she stood uneasy with the tension between them. Finally Winston spoke again and said with his voice a little softer, "It's been a long time." Sarain nodded in agreement, and replied, "About ten years, I think." To Sarain's surprise, Winston gave a slight smile, and said to her, "You haven't aged a day." It was a polite expression, but Sarain knew that his comment was likely to be true with the demon blood coursing through her veins. She pushed the thought to the back of her mind and responded to Winston, "Neither have you, but then I guess that's to be expected."

Winston smiled again, this time a little fuller, in response to Sarain's amusing remark. Suddenly, their conversation was interrupted when Winston's female companion cleared her throat. They both turned and looked at the blond, and then Winston finally thought to say, "Oh, this is Julianne." She turned and looked at Sarain then stated, "I'm his girlfriend."

Sarain quickly examined the woman, she noticed multiple bite marks on her neck, some of them old, and according to Sarain's keen senses, she smelt human. She looked Julianne in the eye and then commented, "You must be his feeding companion." Julianne looked a bit appalled by the statement, but Winston quickly remarked, "How astute of you." Sarain shrugged and replied, "Not really, you always were one to pair up with a feeding companion over hunting... I did find you in the brothel after all." The comment caught Julianne off guard, it was apparent that Winston hadn't shared his whole history with the woman; in fact, she still stared at Sarain with a clueless expression as to who she was.

"I'm Sarain by the way," she told Julianne, but the blond didn't seem familiar with her name. Sarain didn't really care if the girl knew who she was, she never expected for Winston to wait around pining for her, she had abandoned him after all. And with his age, odds were that she was only a small blip in his romantic life.

Sarain then turned to Winston, and said, "I should probably let the two of you go, I'm sure you are busy, and I have things to do myself." She wanted to at least be respectful to Winston, but also felt strange standing there with him and with Julianne as well. He was a part of her past that she had never expected to see again, and looking at him made her feel guilty over how she had treated him. Winston himself seemed a bit awkward, but he nodded in agreement with Sarain, and then remarked, "It was nice seeing you." Sarain knew it was another polite comment, but she felt as though he truly meant it; she believed that Winston wished her well.

Julianne took this moment as a cue to pull Winston away, and together the couple walked past Sarain. Sarain fought the urge to turn around and watch Winston leave; she didn't see him peer over his shoulder as he walked away.

Sarain continued on with her shopping, she went from booth to booth, seeing many strange things. Some looked to be selling charms and potions, others sold ritual garbs, but not a single normal outfit could be found, and the only weapons Sarain saw were engraved, jeweled knives, none of which looked like they would hold up in a fight. Sarain neared the end of her shopping search when she noticed yet another person staring at her, but this one struck her as odd. It appeared to be a man in a hooded cloak, she was sure he was watching her, but she couldn't quite make out his face. She tried not to be obvious about looking, but the man kept managing to keep his face hidden.

Sarain shrugged it off as another curious stranger, and started walking away. After about a minute of walking down the market alleyway, Sarain realized that the cloaked man was following her. She continued to walk as normal, and didn't let on to the fact that she had spotted the man on her tail; there were still many others around, and she doubted the man would make a move on her with so many to witness.

She went to a booth and pretended to exam its items, she picked up a necklace, but as she did so, its pendant came loose and fell to the ground. Sarain bent down to pick it up, and in the moment she looked up she caught a strange feature of the man stalking her. She saw his eyes, his face was still hidden in his shadowy hood, but a flash of yellow gave away that her stalker wasn't human. Sarain instantly thought of Sephor's yellow eyes, but knew that it couldn't be him, she had killed him herself. Whoever this creature was was new to Sarain, but he watched her as though he knew her.

Sarain placed the necklace and its pendant back on the table, and turned to leave. She knew that if a demon's eye color was of a unique shade, then it usually meant it was stronger than a vil sang, and she was without a weapon. She hoped her training wouldn't fail her. She quickly walked down the alley to its exit while trying to devise a plan. She debated waiting in the marketplace until dawn, which wasn't too far away, but she herself didn't want to get caught in the daylight. She thought of going back to her motel, but didn't want the creature to track her scent, especially now that she could no longer setup barriers around her dwellings. And then she thought of Winston, he must live nearby to be out so close to dawn, perhaps she could track him to his home.

Suddenly something came to Sarain's attention; she no longer heard footsteps behind her. She quickly turned around to see the cloaked man missing from the alleyway, and she wondered where he had gone, and if he was still following her. Sarain contemplated going back to her room, but knew that she wasn't quite safe yet. But she also worried about inconveniencing Winston as well as she worried that she might complicate things for him if he wasn't alone.

Sarain took a moment, and then decided to go back to the marketplace; she was going to find Winston. She realized that she might be leading this creature straight to him, but then she also knew that if this creature had been watching all this time, then it would have seen her talking to Winston; she had likely already dragged him into this mess.

Sarain entered back into the marketplace, and immediately headed straight to where she had encountered Winston. She didn't want to draw more attention to herself than she already had with being an outsider, so she pretended to look at booths as she lightly sniffed for a scent; her years of training had unlocked some of her more demonic traits. She recognized the scent of Winston's companion, Julianne, first; her human blood was more potent, and after a little more digging, Sarain caught a hint of a familiar scent, Winston. His smell brought back memories, and she remembered waking up next to him, covered in that scent. She was surprised that she hadn't picked up on it sooner.

Sarain followed his fragrance down the alleyway, with it slowly growing stronger. It wavered from booth to booth, showing that he had stopped to shop at times, but it continued down the alley. Sarain followed the scent to a surprising stop; she stood looking at a dead end. The alleyway ended with a solid brick wall; multiple buildings met, blocking it in. It didn't make sense to her, his trail led her there, and it didn't seem as though he had doubled back; his scent was stronger there than anywhere else in the alleyway.

Sarain began to glance around, and then she decided to double back to the spot she had found Winston at and try again. His scent was getting weak by the time Sarain reached their encounter spot. Now she didn't bother to conceal her actions she searched around, and began asking the vendors if they knew the man she was talking to earlier, but she was met with ignorance and blank stares. She knew these same people had blatantly stared at her earlier, but now that she addressed them, they wouldn't meet her eyes.

She sighed in frustration as she started to head back to the dead end, when the eyes of an old gypsy woman caught her own. The elderly woman stared at her for a second, and then began to wave her over. Sarain approached the woman with caution, and the old lady whispered, "You are looking for your friend are you not?" Sarain nodded, and the woman continued to say, "He lives in Wormwood Alley." The gypsy woman then pointed with a croaked finger back down the alleyway Sarain had come from, and muttered, "It lies that way." Sarain looked at her confused and stated, "But that only leads to a dead end."

The old woman shook her head, and whispered, "The bricks lie… Walk through them and you will find your way." Sarain thought of the vil sang club the X that she had destroyed long ago, and how it had been made to have a glamour illusion to trick humans into not seeing it, perhaps this Wormwood Alley worked the same way, but fooled the eyes of demons and humans alike.

Sarain thanked the elderly woman and turned to leave, when the woman grabbed her by the arm. She then said to Sarain in a hoarse voice, "That isn't a safe place for pretty girls like you, wait until dawn." Sarain pulled her arm away and turned to the woman, saying, "I can handle myself." The woman then reached into her robe and pulled out a rosary, "Take this," Sarain stepped back as the gypsy tried handing it to her. The woman looked up into Sarain's eyes, and immediately placed the rosary back into her robes. "Perhaps not," she muttered to Sarain. The old woman gave Sarain a strange glance as she wandered away from her, and Sarain continued back down the alley.

She hurried to the alley's dead end as quickly as she could for it was nearing dawn. When she reached it she stared at the walls trying to figure out which one was false, but they all looked real. She then extended her hands and felt the bricks; she dragged her fingers along their rough exteriors, and felt nothing abnormal about them. Then she lowered her reach and suddenly saw her hand go through brick; a small portion on the lower wall was an illusion.

Sarain bent down and crawled through the hidden opening, and found darkness on the other side. It was as though she had walked into a building; she glanced around and immediately found a staircase that spiraled down. It was a narrow stairway, and as Sarain stepped down it she realized that it was taking her at least three flights down. She had already been on ground level back up in the alleyway, and she wondered if she was walking into some kind of underground cavern. Then she remembered the old gypsy woman telling her to wait until day, and knew that it couldn't be taking her underground if the time of day had any effect on the place.

Sarain kept a hand on the wall as she traveled down as though waiting for something to happen. She finally stepped down from the last step and was amazed to see desert at the end of her journey. She looked to be in the middle of nowhere, and the landscape looked nothing like the town of Shaven's. In fact, Shaven was nowhere in sight. Sarain saw only a rocky hillside that she knew she would have to climb, since the trail of Winston's scent led her that way.

Sarain headed towards the rocks, and was careful with her footing. She looked up to the sky and saw that the stars had faded and the night sky had turned a dark blue; the sun was soon rising. Sarain made it to the top only to look down and see that she would have to climb down the other side, but she also saw houses along the base. There were just a few, all a distance away from one another and on either side of a dirt road, though the houses looked strange and almost cave-like; they were made of thick stones, and had no windows. Then Sarain realized why this place was hidden and why the gypsy woman had suggested only going there during the day; these were the residences of demons.

Sarain cautiously climbed down the rocky hillside, her footing slipped for a moment as a rock gave out underneath her weight, but her hands grabbed on to the hillside and she held herself up; the rocks digging into the palms of her hands. Her feet finally hit the bottom and Sarain quickly turned around. The sky was growing bluer, and a house caught Sarain's eyes. It looked just like all the others, but the difference was that Winston's scent was coming from it; he must currently be inside.

Sarain loudly called out Winston's name as she approached his house, but she was still a ways away. She was just barely leaving the hillside, and still had to cross the wide dirt road, but it didn't take long for him to come to the door. The door opened and a curious Winston peered out, but he stayed in his doorway, it was nearly dawn.

"What are you doing here?" he called out then quickly changed his tone to defensive when asking; "Did you follow me?" "No, it's not like that," Sarain immediately said, and she heard Winston muttered to himself, "I thought I covered my tracks." Sarain explained, "I didn't follow 'you', I followed your scent."

Winston laughed and immediately stated, "Impossible, I don't care how good of a hunter you are, no human can follow a scent that well... How long have you really been out here?"

Sarain opened her mouth to explain when a screeching sound caused her to turn around. She saw a gray skinned man flying at her with bat like wings and bright yellow eyes, and she realized how her stalker managed to disappear so quickly; he could fly. Before Sarain could react, the strange demon swooped down and grabbed her, lifting her into the air. Sarain heard Winston yell out her name from down below as she struggled in the air with the beast. It had a tight grip on her with its talon claws digging into her skin. She stared into its yellow eyes, and saw that though it had the body of a monster it still had the face of a man.

The creature returned Sarain's gaze and said to her in almost an animalistic voice, "It looks as though the prodigal child has returned." "Is that what this is? You're trying to return me to my father?" Sarain demanded, but the beast gave her an evil glare and stated, "I don't want him to ever find you!" Sarain looked at the creature confused and he smiled as he remarked, "Not all of the Sangre de Hermandad want to see you leading by your father's side." "The what?" Sarain muttered as she struggled with the beast.

She twisted and turned feeling her heart race and her body becoming unusually cold. The beast looked down at her and quickly stated, "That's enough of that!" And he suddenly let her go. Sarain wasn't sure if she had slipped out of its grip or if the thing had thrown her, but she quickly felt her body rushing toward the ground.

Sarain waited for the inevitable hard thud when landing on the rocks, but was surprised when her landing was cushioned, her breath not even getting knocked out of her. She looked up in a haze and saw Winston staring down at her, he had caught her. Sarain's head was spinning, likely from her fast drop from a high altitude, and she saw that the sky looked gray. She gazed up at Winston, dizzily, and remarked, "You feel warm." Winston laughed and said, "You must be cold."

Suddenly and without warning, Sarain felt a surge of pain go through her body, and she jerked and began to convulse. Winston lost his hold on her, and Sarain went tumbling to the ground, her hair flipping over her face. He immediately went to her aid; he bent down and gently brushed the hair away from her face, and then suddenly gasped. Sarain's violet eyes were illuminated and fangs were in her mouth. Winston cried out, "Who did this to you?"

Sarain did not answer, but continued to convulse. She heard in the distance a feminine voice call out, "Hurry! The sun is coming up." Then she felt Winston lift her up and run as he carried her. She caught a glimpse of a sun ray coming near them, but lost the image and consciousness a moment later.

Chapter 3

Sarain began to open her eyes slowly, she caught a glimpse of Winston holding up her arm, and he appeared to be cleaning the blood off her wounds. She felt the weight of many blankets on her, and realized that Winston must have tried to make her warm. She heard him say, "That's strange," and then a woman's voice asked, "What?" He answered the woman, "Her wounds have already healed." "Isn't that normal with your kind?" the woman asked. "No, not like this. That's too quick," Winston replied.

Sarain grunted and began to lift her head, she saw Julianne in the room with them. Winston turned to Sarain and said, "No, don't sit up, you need to lie down." But Sarain didn't comply; she sat up with a groan, and looked around the room. She was in Winston's home, and it was dark, barely lit by candles.

She heard Winston ask again, "Who did this to you?" And without thinking she muttered, "No one." "Was it a demon?" he asked ignoring her first answer, thinking she was still incoherent, "You healed faster than a normal vil sang." Sarain groaned in frustration, and said again, "It was no one." Sarain began to lift herself up to stand, but Winston immediately pushed her down, demanding, "No, you need to rest."

Sarain swatted at his arm, and struggled to get up again, but this time Winston moved both his hands to her shoulders, and forced her down. "Stop being so stubborn!" he told her. Sarain then screeched and twisted underneath him, her head still pounding. She tried to knock him away, and she heard Julianne ask, "What's wrong with her?" With a surge of energy, Sarain threw Winston back, and she jumped up and ran for the door. He quickly tackled her to the ground, grabbing her by the shirt. The sound of cloth ripping echoed out, and suddenly Winston hollered.

He looked to his arm to see an ankh shaped burn scar, and immediately said, "What the hell?" Winston then glanced at Sarain to see that beneath her shirt, now hanging out from the torn fabric, was the ankh she had always worn. He backed away from her while muttering, "How?"

A look of fear came over Sarain's eyes and she turned to head for the door. Instantaneously, both Winston and Julianne call out, "No!" in hopes of stopping Sarain. Winston reached out to grab her, but missed. Sarain flung open the door and ran out into the sun. She looked back at Winston cowering inside his dark home as she stood safely in the sunlight, then she turned and ran away.

Julianne shut the door, and stared down at Winston with confusion, "I don't understand, I thought she was like you." Winston shook his head slowly still in shock and muttered, "No, she's something else."

Sarain's burst of energy soon died down, and she dragged her way back to the Scarlet Motel. The sun was high by the time she reached it, and she was tired. With her all-night adventure and her long bus ride, the demonic seizure really wore Sarain out. She went to the large red bed, and collapsed upon it. She didn't care how grimy it looked, she needed rest. She closed her eyes as she lay on her back, not daring to look up into the lewd mirror hanging above the bed. She couldn't handle any more surprises; running into Winston was already more than she bargained for, and this new yellow eyed demon; not even in town for twenty-four hours and already someone wanted her dead. But it wasn't this odd new type of demon that worried Sarain, it was the way Winston looked at her when he was caring over her, and it was the way she felt about it.

Sarain watched as the demons retreated, and realized that dawn was approaching. She climbed out of her crate and over the dead body of the demon she had just killed. She glanced over at her grandfather's bones, and felt her stomach churn; she was only thirteen, but she was now alone in the world.

Sarain then turned her gaze to the body of her friend, Orran. He laid face down and she saw a small pool of blood forming around him. She looked down at her friend as her vision blurred with warm tears falling from her eyes and rolling down her cheeks. Sarain stared down at him, the image burning into her mind. She shut her eyes and suddenly Sephor slashing Orran across the chest and biting his throat flashed into her head. Sarain then turned, bent down, and vomited on the ground. She wiped her mouth, and looked back at her friend, thinking, she would do anything for him to suddenly get up, but she knew that wasn't possible.

It was then Sarain heard rustling coming from nearby, and her first thought was, the demons were coming back. It was close to dawn, but the sun wasn't out yet. Sarain was lucky to have killed one beast, but she couldn't fight an army. She only had one choice she could make, and that was to run. Sarain gave Orran's body one last look, and felt sorry that she couldn't give him a proper burial. Finally she turned away and ran across the field and into the woods; opposite from where she had seen the demons flee. She never turned around, and didn't dare go back for Orran's body.

It would be a long time before she would ever feel safe again, even in the sunlight.

Sarain woke to a dark room; she had slept the day away. She still felt tired, but her body felt better, stronger. She stretched and started to groan, but immediately shot up in bed when a figure caught her attention. Someone was sitting on the edge of her bed. Her eyes lit up in defense and her fangs began to descend when a voice suddenly said, "Stop!" And Sarain complied when she recognized the voice as Winston's. His own eyes were glowing now, the same vibrant blue glow that she remembered from years ago. She wondered why she hadn't recognized him right away, but realized that her eyes may be quick to adjust to the dark, but still took a while to adjust from sleep.

"You followed my scent?" Sarain asked. "Yes, and no, actually, there's not many motels in town. Your scent had already faded during the day, but after checking the few motels around, I smelled your scent coming out from under your door," Winston explained.

"Oh," Sarain simply muttered, and clutched the blankets to her chest. Winston stared at her for a moment before saying, "Aren't we going to talk about what happened back there?" Sarain sat in silence, avoiding his gaze, so Winston spoke again, asking, "Why did you run?" "I panicked," Sarain mumbled. "Yeah, I got that... Why?" he continued to pry.

Sarain looked down and muttered, "I didn't want to drag you into all of this... My life, it's gotten complicated." "Your life has always been complicated... But that's never stopped me before," Winston told her, and smiled. His expression then changed again and he looked solemn as he asked, "About the other thing... The seizure you had, does it happen often?" "From time to time," she replied. "That's what happens when your body is changing into a vil sang, it usually lasts for a few days. I'm surprised you can still wear that ankh and walk in the sun if your eyes and teeth are already changing," Winston relayed, and then asked, "How long has it been happening?"

"Seven years," Sarain answered. Winston's eyes went wide, and he looked confused, so Sarain explained further, "I didn't get infected by a demon if that's what you think... I was born this way; it just took time to surface." Winston was quiet for a minute, and then said, "I'm not sure how it's possible, but I believe you... Either way, this place isn't safe for you." Sarain sat and asked, "What, why not?"

Winston then gave her an odd stare as he said, "Really? Come on, I snuck in here while you were sleeping; anyone or anything can do that as well." "And where do you suppose I stay?" Sarain asked sarcastically. "With me," he answered. Sarain laughed then remarked, "I'm sure your girlfriend would love that!" Winston glared at her and stated, "I'm serious... Now you've already dragged me into this, the least you could do is let me help you."

"Like your place is so much safer, I got attacked right outside it!" Sarain proclaimed. "Exactly," Winston said in frustration, "And what if that thing comes back looking for you? Do you want me there all by my lonesome?" Sarain looked at him confused, "Wait; now you want me to protect you?" Winston sighed and said, "What I'm trying to say is that we work better as a team." He stood up and continued, "It's obvious that you're going to need my help, that demon risked getting caught in the daylight to attack you," Winston then extended a hand to Sarain, "Let me help you."

Sarain thought it over, the demon had flown into the predawn to grab her, but Winston had also run out into it to save her. She looked up at him, and knew that if she could trust anyone that it was him.

Sarain took Winston's hand and left with him.

Chapter 4

Winston opened the door for Sarain once they arrived at his place, he had also offered to carry her one small bag, but she refused to let him. His gentlemanly act made her feel uneasy, but she didn't know why. She walked into his place and felt out of place in it, she remembered how he had once preferred to stay in lavish conditions like the Velvet Rose, but his home now was humble.

Sarain turned toward Winston and asked, "Where exactly will I be staying?" "In my bedroom," he replied, and Sarain's eyes immediately bulged in shock. Winston chuckled at her reaction and stated, "Don't worry; I'll be staying in here." He still had a smirk on his face as he walked past Sarain to show her the way. The room wasn't far, mostly because his house wasn't big, and when Winston walked into the room, he immediately took out a sheet to cover the mirror that hung above his dresser.

Sarain looked at him with surprise and said, "You remembered." Winston smiled again and replied, "How could I forget such a strange request?" He then began to cover the mirror when he caught a glimpse of something strange; there was a dark mist around Sarain. He then looked back at her as she was bent down placing her bag on the floor, and he saw no such mist. Winston turned back to the mirror and the reflection was fine; he had never seen anything odd in mirrors before, and thought that maybe it was only his eyes playing tricks on him as he tugged the sheet over and around the mirror.

He turned back to Sarain who had plopped herself down on the bed, a look of concern on her face. "What is it?" Winston asked. Sarain shook her head slightly and replied, "I don't know, just something that demon said." She then looked up at him and asked, "Have you ever heard of Sangre de Hermandad?" "The Brotherhood of Blood," Winston responded, "That's the last group you want to get involved with." He then looked down at Sarain with worry, and asked, "Is that who's after you? Can I ask why?"

Sarain took a deep breath and replied, "I think my father might be their leader." Winston looked at her with shock, and he managed to ask, "What is your father exactly?" Sarain gazed up at him and answered, "An Ancient." Winston suddenly sat down on the bed next to her, staring down at the ground and muttering, "I didn't know that those things actually existed." "Well apparently being the offspring of one is even rarer, I think that's why these guys want to kill me," Sarain explained. Winston turned to Sarain confused, "But if the leader is your father then why does he want you dead?" "I don't know why, but I'm not sure that he's the one who does. That demon just said that not everyone wanted to see me leading by my father's side," she replied.

Winston nearly chuckled with amusement as he commented, "Like you would ever lead a demon army." Sarain smirked and turned to Winston, saying, "I know, seriously, who would have guessed that things would have ended up like this. And after all that hunting and training, I wind up a demon myself." Sarain laughed and then began to cry.

Winston quickly turned to Sarain when he heard the change in her tone. He saw tears running down her face, and instinctively he put his arms around Sarain. He placed his hand on her back as he said, "Don't cry, being a demon really isn't that bad; we don't all lose ourselves." "At least you had a choice," Sarain muttered, and then Winston replied, "Knowing that I chose this life only makes it worse." Then he was quiet for a moment, he took a deep breath, and began to say, "But at least one good thing came from all of this…"

The bedroom door suddenly creaked and both Sarain and Winston looked up to see Julianne standing in the doorway, and looking very displeased. Winston abruptly let go of Sarain, and stood up. He walked over to Julianne while Sarain remained seated. Sarain could see that Julianne was upset, but she felt as though she had done nothing wrong; she had not asked for Winston to take her in nor did she make him hold her. Besides, to her, they were just friends. Surely Winston felt the same way. Then Sarain looked up and saw the guilty look on his face, and then she felt a little guilty herself.

Sarain looked away as Winston told Julianne a vague version of what was going on that ended with him telling her that Sarain would be staying with him. Julianne seemed angry, but she didn't say anything in return. After things calmed down some, Sarain looked up at the couple and said, "I hate to interrupt…" she then quickly glanced down at her tattered shirt, and said, "But I kind of need a change of clothes."

Julianne gazed over at her, expressionless, and simply replied, "I have something here that you can wear."

A little while later Sarain came out of the bedroom wearing a pink puppy shirt and a frown. Winston looked up as she entered the room and immediately began laughing. She shot him a dirty look and quickly said, "It's not funny," then she asked, "Julianne didn't have any grown up clothes, or does she just hate me?" Winston stopped laughing and they both got quiet, and then Sarain asked, "Where is she by the way?"

"She left while you were changing," he replied. "She didn't stay very long… She didn't have to leave on my account, if that's what it was," Sarain remarked. Winston shook his head and stated, "No, it's not like that, she's… just a busy person." The pause in Winston's sentence and the look on his face as he said it told Sarain that there was much more going on than he was telling her, but she didn't want to pry into his love life.

Sarain quickly looked down at her shirt, breaking the awkward moment, and stated, "We need to go shopping quick."

An hour later Sarain found herself standing under a fluorescent light with Winston by her side as she thumbed through clothing. It was one of the few stores left open at that hour; it was a second hand store, no weapons, just clothes and knick-knacks. There was something oddly amusing about the scene; two unnatural creatures, both with blood-stained pasts, and their own histories formally entwined. Who with all the battling they have faced and likely would face, there they were shopping for clothes like ordinary people, friends even.

Sarain grabbed what little dark casual clothing she could find in her size. She turned to Winston, and saw him holding up a skimpy red dress, one that looked like it should be worn by a street walker. A look came over Sarain's face as her eyes took in the outfit, and immediately she said, "I am not wearing that!"

A grin spread across Winston's face as he replied, "But if you did, you wouldn't have to worry about hunting down demons; they would come to you in this little number." Sarain rolled her eyes and sarcastically remarked, "Maybe you should get it for Julianne." Winston turned away as he put back the dress and muttered under his breath, "She couldn't pull it off." Sarain looked at him through the corner of her eye and wondered if Winston realized that her hearing had grown along with her strength. She ignored the comment, and purchased her items.

They walked out of the store silently with Sarain carrying a plastic bag of clothes, and all the while feeling strange; Winston was one of the last people Sarain pictured herself doing such a mundane task with, especially after all they had been through, but as she turned and glimpsed Winston, seeing him staring back at her made her feel less odd.

A sudden rustle in nearby bushes immediately grabbed both of their attentions. Winston quickly asked Sarain, "Do you have a weapon?" "No," she muttered as she positioned herself to run. Winston prepared himself to run as well, and when a beast leaped out of the bushes at them, he was surprised to see Sarain run, not away, but towards the demon. She lunged at the creature, and leapt onto it like a cat. The demon was large and gray, its skin looked damp and bumpy like a greased up bodybuilder. It was easily three times Sarain's size, but this didn't concern her as Sarain pounded her fists against the monster's hard flesh.

Winston watched for a moment, debating on what to do, and immediately went into action when he saw the creature throw Sarain off its back. Winston caught her like a reflex, and Sarain was instantly back on her feet. Winston heard Sarain call out, "Why were you following us?" to the creature, and he wondered if she had known the demon was there all along. The beast didn't reply, but swung its clawed hand at Sarain, and she quickly ducked it.

Sarain punched the demon in the chest, and Winston saw its skin crack like a shell. He was aware that some demons had a very hard exoskeleton, and was amazed to see Sarain so easily punching through it; her strength really had grown. The punch seemed to stun the creature so she quickly swept its feet out from under it and the beast fell onto its back. Sarain leapt onto its chest, and slammed the demon's head rapidly against the ground.

She repeated her question, "Why were you following us?" The creature groaned in pain, and with a hoarse voice, muttered, "Kayne." "Kayne?" Sarain repeated, and slammed the beast's head again. The demon began to cough up black blood, as he struggled to say, "Orders." It came out like a gurgle, and Sarain knew that the creature was no longer good to talk.

She suddenly punched her fist through the beast's chest, and it stopped moving. She pulled out her hand, and Winston saw that it and halfway to her elbow was completely covered in black sludgy blood. He had seen Sarain kill Sephor in a similar fashion, but that was while channeling all her strength; now Sarain seemed as though she had barely even broken a sweat.

Sarain got up off of the demon's lifeless body and quickly turned to Winston. Her eyes were glowing and her mouth was shifted in an awkward position; Winston knew that Sarain was hiding her fangs from him. He looked down at the beast for a second, and then back up at Sarain, thinking that he couldn't have killed that demon that easily, and that he likely would have needed a weapon.

Winston began to wonder about the strength of an Ancient; if it could make Sarain as strong as she was without being fully demonic, then how strong was the creature itself, and did the two of them really stand a chance going up against it and its brotherhood?

Sarain saw the peculiar look on Winston's face as he stared at her, and she felt odd once again. She turned away from his gaze, picked up her bag, and muttered, "Let's go back to your house."

Her eyes were wide and staring straight as she watched the bloody blade pull out of her lover's back. A pool of blood quickly formed on his shirt as the life in his eyes began to slip away. His eyes went glassy as he stared out to her, but his gaze wasn't one of fear or helplessness; it was one of betrayal. She had failed him, and no love reflected from his eyes.

His body slumped forward and he fell, face first. She wanted to rush to him, but she realized that she couldn't move. She screamed out her lover's name, and heard her own fear echoing throughout the empty room.

His killer slowly moved toward her with her body still frozen. The murderer moved in twitchy shifts, as though walking under a strobe light. Its body was dark and shadowy, and its image appeared out of focus. The murderer knelt down before her, and as she looked into its violet eyes she saw a familiar face.

As she had already guessed, her father's face stared back at her, but as his body blurred and shifted, so did his face. The eyes did not change, but the beholder did.

Sarain's breath caught in her throat, and it felt as though the air was being sucked out of her. She stared at his new face, and didn't understand; the one staring back at her was her own. Her image appeared to be a perfect clone, at first glance, but something didn't feel right about it; besides the terror of looking into one's own face, the portions of it seemed slightly off. The hue of her skin wasn't right either; it was too pale, almost gray even.

Her clone smiled at her, exposing a mouth full of razor sharp teeth, and lips that seemed to stretch too wide. It leaned in closer to Sarain, its eyes illuminating as she watched its skin harden into a shell, and its features becoming more demonic. It moved its lips to her ear, and she felt its icy cold breath against her skin as it whispered, "In time..."

Sarain shot up in bed, covered in sweat, her heart pounding, her skin pulsating, and every ounce of her being ready to fight. She had been dreaming, but the nightmare wasn't over as she heard the creature's final words echoing in her ears.

"In time... you'll be me."

Chapter 5

The room was dark, and felt hot and sticky from the frantic energy Sarain must have unleashed during her nightmare. Her hand went up to wipe the sweat from her brow, just as Winston suddenly burst into the room. She gazed up at him with puzzlement, and quickly noticed the look of alarm on his face.

"Are you alright?" he asked while panting, he must have raced to her aide. Sarain nodded her head, and muttered, "Nightmare," then she asked him with curiosity as her mind began to clear, "How did you know something was wrong?" Winston stared at her almost in shock as he replied, "You were screaming 'Orran' at the top of your lungs!"

Sarain looked down in confusion, she had been dreaming about Eddie's death, and could have sworn she had called out his name in the dream, but once again while trying to think of him her thoughts must have wandered to Orran. She felt guilt hit the pit of her stomach, and she wondered if that was why Eddie's eyes always looked so betrayed in her dreams, because he was never the one she was truly grieving for.

Sarain's heart began racing again, and she tried to ignore it. For a moment she thought her body was having a surge of demonic energy, but when her teeth didn't descend, she realized that the stress on her body wasn't physical, but emotional; she was having a panic attack.

She looked away from Winston, and started to turn her head just as a tear escaped her eye, and it didn't go unnoticed. Winston's eyes went wide and he quickly moved toward Sarain, saying, "Something's wrong." Her hand went up to hide her eyes, but he grabbed her arm and stopped her. "You're crying," he observed then he wiped her tear away, and said, "You don't have to hide yourself from me. I could never think less of you."

Sarain turned and gazed at Winston in amazement; she then leaned toward him and wrapped her arms around him. She pressed herself against him tightly in a hug, and Winston was caught off guard. Another tear fell from her eyes, but this one was out of relief; relief to know that for once she had a friend that she could go to.

After a long moment, Sarain finally pulled herself away, and as she slowly brought her head back, she felt the cold skin of Winston's cheek graze against hers. She continued to pull away from him, but as his eyes gazed down until they met hers, he stopped her from letting go of him. She saw his blue eyes settle onto her lips, and when he began to lean in, Sarain muttered a single word, "Julianne."

Winston stopped himself before he could touch her, and he let Sarain slip out from his grasp. He knew that with everything Sarain was that she could never be the other woman, and he could never force her to.

Sarain woke up dazed and sudden when she heard the sounds of a woman shouting. She lifted her head from the bed with a groan, and recognized the voice as Julianne's. She checked her watch to see that it was in the middle of the day, a bit of an odd time to visit a vil sang, but not entirely strange. Sarain was curious as to why Julianne was shouting so she went to the bedroom door and cracked it open. She heard Julianne yell, "What do you mean 'we've grown apart'? Everything was fine not even a week ago, before 'she' came!"

Sarain closed the door when she realized that Julianne was talking about her, and that it sounded like she and Winston were breaking up. Sarain thought of how Winston had almost kissed her the night before, she had thought that it might have just been him being impulsive and in the moment, but now she was beginning to see that perhaps having her back in his life was making him want to rekindle the past. Sarain didn't know how she felt about that, she did care for Winston, but her new found friendship with him still felt delicate. She wasn't sure if their friendship could survive another romantic interlude.

Sarain quickly dressed then sat down and waited on the edge of the bed. When the front door slammed shut, Sarain knew it was only a matter of time before Winston came knocking. Almost on cue, a soft knock came against the door, and Winston asked, "Can I come in?"

Sarain got up and let him in with Winston quickly saying, "I guess you probably heard all that… Sorry for the ruckus, I hope it didn't wake you." "Don't worry about it," Sarain muttered not looking Winston in the eye, and she asked, "Is everything okay?" He hesitated a moment before responding, and when he did he answered, "Yes, except Julianne won't be coming around anymore."

Sarain was quiet as she thought of how to respond, she wasn't an expert when it came to relationships or words of comfort, so she said what she knew, "Well, I would imagine all relationships between a human and a demon would be doomed. Someone would inevitably grow old and die, or hate the other one for turning them and leading them down a road of darkness… Humans are fragile, they aren't meant for this life, if Julianne would have stayed, she probably would have hated you for your youth and strength, and mostly for all the misery that surrounds us."

A sad expression came over Winston's face as he gazed at Sarain. When she wouldn't meet his stare he remarked to her, "It sounds like you're speaking from experience." She turned her back to him and her eye caught the picture of Orran and her as teenagers peeking out of her bag, and then she muttered, "A lot happened since you last knew me."

Winston didn't pry, but instead remained silent, it was Sarain who broke the awkwardness by saying, "Besides, she was too young for you." "Technically, you were too young for me too," Winston stated almost with a smirk. "Yeah, and look how well that turned out," Sarain immediately remarked, and then realized it came out harsher than she had intended it to.

The room was silent again, and Sarain muttered, "I need to wash up." She quickly left the room leaving Winston there to wonder if he had done something wrong that put her on edge. He began to turn to leave the room himself when he noticed the picture hanging out of Sarain's bag. His curiosity got the better of him and he knelt down to look at the picture. He became slightly amused when he saw the young and awkward looking Sarain in the photograph. He began to smile at the cuteness he saw in her image, and when he flipped the photo over he saw the date and 'Orran' written on the back, and he realized that he was a friend Sarain had lost when her clan was murdered.

Winston immediately put the photo back in Sarain's bag, and felt guilty for having looked at it. He headed for the door, and then stopped when he began to wonder why of all people, Sarain would call the name out of a boy who died seventeen years ago. It was strange, by the way she acted he had thought she had lost this 'Orran' more recently.

"Was she in love with him?" Winston thought to himself then he shrugged the thought away, and left the room.

Later, Sarain found Winston waiting for her in his
den. The sun was nearly set, and the first thing Sarain
said when seeing him was, "We need to get some
weapons." She relayed how the beast she had fought the
night before had mentioned someone named 'Kayne' and
'orders' that likely meant more demons would be
coming. Since she had been followed to his house once
before, they had to be prepared to be attacked there again.
She suggested stocking up on blades strong enough to
withstand striking against stone, many possible beasts
they could fight would likely have strong shell-like skin.

"You're not going to find weapons like that in a
store around here," Winston stated. "Then we go out of
town for them," Sarain started to say, but Winston
abruptly remarked, "Wait, you didn't let me finish. What
I meant to say is that a 'regular' store wouldn't carry
them; the marketplace will."

Sarain gave him a look of puzzlement and said, "I
didn't see any weapons like that when I was there."
"That's because you were looking in the wrong place," he
explained.

Winston told her that there were other places
around town and in the marketplace, which were hidden
like how the passage to his home is. The town of Shaven
was small, but it was only a front for a demonic city. Not
all the demons that resided in it were evil; fact was a lot
of them lived in peace with one another, and this city
allowed them to connect and coexist. Winston explained

that many of the humans there were aware of the demonic life in the town, and often helped them maintain a humane society structure. Providing demons with blood and cover from hunters, a lot of the human residents also dabbled in the occult, and relied on the mystic energy that radiated from this particular land. Shaven was a secret gathering place for many of the supernatural kind. It sounded like the picture perfect place for Aion to take cover in.

Winston led Sarain back to the marketplace, and when they got there he led her to two particular booths that stood side by side. The booths weren't what he was interested in, but instead it was the gap between them. Winston took a hold of Sarain's hand and brought it up to the brick of the building the booths sat against, and she felt that the bricks there between the booths were false like the ones leading to Wormwood Alley.

Together they stepped through the false bricks and into a tunnel. The tunnel stretched long and was dimly lit by a few mere candles. Sarain thought it odd to use candles to light such a long tunnel, and as if reading her mind, Winston leaned in toward her and whispered, "The candles never burn out."

They proceeded down the tunnel, and Sarain noticed a light glowing at the other end. As they walked, Winston muttered to Sarain, "Doesn't this remind you of the tunnels underneath The Purge?" It did in fact remind her of them, and the thought brought a smile to her face; she hated that place, but liked that she could talk to someone that actually knew and remembered things from her past, she didn't have to hide anything from Winston.

They came upon the end of the tunnel, and it led them to a room with a few booths set up. The first booth they went to was manned by a tall shadowy figure in a hooded cloak. The figure stood about seven feet tall and very thin, and from it came the voice of a man, but Sarain wasn't sure if that was what it was. It appeared to know Winston when it remarked, "No Julianne today?"

"No, I won't be coming here with her anymore," Winston replied. Then the creature turned and glanced at Sarain, an orange glow caught her eye, and she heard it say, "I see you're keeping company with your own kind for once." Sarain wasn't sure if she was more surprised that the creature immediately recognized her as not human, or if it was by the fact that Winston didn't much associate with other demons. Winston always did have the habit of still acting like a man regardless of what he really was.

Winston quickly glanced at Sarain and then said to the creature, "She's an old friend." It nodded at him and replied, "She looks very special; powerful. You should keep her by your side." Sarain felt a bit embarrassed and confused, and when Winston led her away from the booth, he whispered in her ear, "He can see auras."

They moved to the next booth where laid out on a table were swords and knives. This booth was manned by what appeared to be a man, but Sarain noticed that he didn't have a scent, and normally both humans and vil sangs gave off smells. She wasn't sure what he was. Winston explained to the man what they were looking for in a weapon, and he pointed out two swords and a knife to them.

"These three are magically blessed, they will hold and do what you need them to," the man said. "We'll take them," Winston quickly replied, and asked, "What is the payment?" The man gazed at Sarain intently, and answered, "A drop of her blood." Winston's expression turned to one of appall, and he quickly said, "No!" But Sarain looked the man in his eyes, and answered, "Yes." Winston turned to her and asked, "Are you sure?" She nodded and said, "I can spare a drop."

The man brought out a silvery needle and a small clear vial, and then took a hold of Sarain's hand. He brought the tip of the needle to her index finger, and lightly pricked it. Sarain then placed her finger at the opening of the vial, and squeezed out a single drop of blood. The man sealed the vial and gave a quick examination to the content inside. "Powerful stuff indeed; this will fetch a good price," he remarked and then placed the vial away. Next, he took out a few yards of cloth, and wrapped the blades up inside, he then tied the cloth shut with ribbon and handed them the blades.

Winston gave the man a distrusting look, but took the blades. He then turned to Sarain, and said, "Let's get out of here." They strapped the clothed swords to their backs, and Sarain tucked the knife into her boot.

They headed back down the tunnel, and after they were a little bit away from the room Winston glanced at Sarain's hand and asked, "Are you alright?" She gave him a puzzled look, and then stated, "You've seen me get stabbed in the back, and you're worried about a little needle prick?" Winston almost smiled from her comment, and then said, "I know, I just always worry about you." Sarain glanced at Winston from the corner of her eye to see him staring at her. A moment of silence went by, and then Winston sighed, causing Sarain to ask, "What is it?"

"Are we going to talk about what happened last night?" he said with frustration. "Nothing happened last night," Sarain remarked, and then she noticed that Winston had stopped walking, so she turned around to face him. "We almost kissed... the only thing that stopped us was Julianne, and now she's not a factor anymore," he recounted. Sarain took a deep breath and contemplated how to react to Winston's statement, and then she said, "You always have to put me on the spot."

Sarain started to walk again when Winston called out, "If I didn't, I would never get anything from you!" She quickly turned around again and stated, "Why do you need anything from me?" He stared at her for a moment as though the answer should have been obvious then he answered her by saying, "You know I can't be around you and not be with you... That has never changed, and that's why I didn't go looking for you after you left."

"Because I was the horrible one who abandoned you," Sarain said sarcastically. "No, because you needed time to figure out if you could spend your life with a creature like me," he remarked, and added, "It looks like fate stepped in for you; you'll have to deal with a demonic lifestyle whether you want to or not, and you found me whether or not you were looking." Sarain glanced over at Winston silently, and he said to her, "You need to decide if you still want to run away from what we have?"

She stared at him a moment longer then stated, "Let's just go back to the house."

They stepped out from the tunnel, Winston following behind, and a cool night breeze rushed through Sarain's hair. As they walked through the marketplace, she reflected over Winston's words, and then suddenly stopped in place. Winston turned to her confused and a bit annoyed as he asked, "What is it now?"

Sarain looked up at the stars and muttered, "You always put me on the spot…" "You said that," he commented. Then Sarain looked to Winston and asked, "And what if I am ready?" He stared at her half puzzled and half intrigued, as he asked, "Ready for what?" "Ready for you and me," she replied.

Winston took a step closer to Sarain; he gazed down at her and muttered, "Seriously?" She stared up him, looking into his blue eyes, and started to stretch up, when movement from the corner of her eye slightly caught her attention. Sarain could feel Winston's cool breath on her skin as she longed to feel the softness of his lips, but she froze and then pulled away when she realized what it was exactly that was trying to steal her

48

attention away from him. Her breath caught in her throat, and she let out a gasp. Her heart nearly stopped and she heard herself say, "Oh my god."

Winston looked down at her baffled, and then quickly followed her gaze. He turned to see a man standing near them and baring a scar on his neck, and the man was watching Sarain intensively.

Sarain continued to stare on in disbelief as if hypnotized, and only managed to mutter out one word, "Orran."

Chapter 6

His skin was tanned, his hair was dark and long, and his eyes were hazel. He was older than she remembered him, and bore a nasty scar on his neck. He had other cuts and scrapes about him that made her realize that he was still a hunter. He didn't resemble Eddie as much as she thought he would have, but Sarain was certain she was looking at her old friend, Orran.

He took a slow and curious step closer to her, and squinted to get a better look. She looked up at him with wide child-like eyes, that when he gazed upon her face, a look of recognition came over his, and he spoke softly, "Sarain."

Her heart began to race, as she quickly brushed past Winston, and ran to her long lost friend. She collided with Orran, wrapping her arms around him, and slightly knocking him back. He was caught off guard, but after a moment, wrapped his own arms around her, and rested his chin upon her head.

Tears welled in Sarain's eyes as she stammered out, "I thought you were dead." Orran closed his eyes as he held her, saying, "I thought I lost you too." The old friends held onto each other as if clinging to their lost childhoods, oblivious to the world, and the glare of Winston's building rage as he became aware of whom the man was.

After a few minutes, Sarain loosened her grip on Orran, and then finally took a step back. Orran took a deep breath and said, "Finally I can breathe again," and then he looked down at his friend with a smirk on his face. His smile brought Sarain's childhood flooding back; that same smile always on his face when he looked at her. She smiled back at him, and then suddenly thought to ask, "What are you doing here?" "Same reason I imagine you are here for," he said, and then he whispered, "Hunting, for the things that killed our clan….. The trail led you here too, right?"

"Umm…yeah, but how….how did you survive?" Sarain asked, staring up at him curiously. Orran took a quick glimpse around them, and then replied, "Not here; it isn't safe." And then suddenly Winston approached Orran saying, "Come on, we can go back to my place." Orran stared at him suspiciously, but Sarain quickly stated, "It's okay, he can be trusted." Orran gave Winston another quick glance, and said, "Alright."

Sarain then led the way with Orran in tow. Winston followed behind; making sure no one was trailing them. Every now and then he glimpsed ahead, checking to see how closely Orran was staying to Sarain. He didn't like it when she took his hand to help steady their way up and down the steep hill near his house.

Orran followed them back without question, and didn't seem surprised or even curious to the path that led to Winston's house. Sarain imagined that just like her, Orran must have seen and experienced many strange things in the years they had been apart. Seventeen years was a long time, but as Sarain stared over at Orran, it felt like nothing had changed with her old friend. But then she realized, she had changed, whether it was obvious to Orran or not, Sarain was not the girl she once was, and she was unsure if he would be able to deal with what she was becoming.

Sarain shook the thought out of her head, and once again wallowed in the amazement of her reunion, and continued to lead Orran to her new found safe-house. When they arrived Winston let them in, and Orran didn't question why the house had no windows; to a hunter, they only made a room less secure since they could be made into another possible entry point to a demon.

After entering the house they sat around the den where Sarain asked once again, "How did you survive the raid on our clan?" "I could ask you the same thing," Orran immediately said, but then he answered her by explaining, "After that large demonic vil sang bit me, I blacked out, when I came through, I was in a hospital being treated for anemia. I was found by hunters that occasionally did business with our clan… They told me that they found no other survivors; I had assumed that you were amongst the other bodies that they buried. And since, I've been hunting for the things that were behind the attack that night. I've come across and killed a few of the demons, but I still don't know why it happened, and I haven't been able to find the one that murdered most of our clan and bit me."

Winston quickly looked at Sarain and muttered, "Sephor?" And Sarain nodded to him. Orran noticed the interaction and asked, "What is it?" Sarain then looked at him and said, "I killed that demon ten years ago." Orran stared at her blankly for a moment, stunned, and then finally said, "Well it seems that I've wasted a lot of effort over the past few years... You haven't destroyed them all have you?" Sarain shook her head, "No, but I'm working on it." Orran was quiet for a while before asking, "Do you know why it happened?"

Sarain didn't answer right away, instead she gave a quick glance to Winston, who gave her a slight nod as if knowing what she was silently asking of him before she answered Orran with a lie; "No." He sighed with disappointment then asked, "How did you survive that night?" "I ran," she simply said.

Sarain looked over at her old friend, still amazed to see him sitting across from her, and didn't realize she was staring until Orran remarked, "Is there something on my face?" She slightly blushed, but honestly replied, "I thought you were dead." "I know," he muttered softly, "I thought you died too." Sarain shook her head and stated, "No, I really thought I saw you die. When you got slashed across the chest and my gasp caused you to hesitate, and you got bit. I thought you died; I thought I got you killed."

A look of recall came over Orran's face as he said, "So that was you." Sarain felt herself get hit with a pang of guilt that must have been visible on her face, because Orran immediately said, "That wasn't your fault…I just wish that I could have protected you better, maybe then you wouldn't have had to run…And we wouldn't have had to be alone all these years." His words overwhelmed Sarain, and she felt as though she once again had family; she missed his protective wing.

Winston sat there in the den amongst them, but felt as though he might as well been watching from a distance; either way he felt like an outcast, and that he didn't need to be near to see the obvious closeness of the two old friends. He glanced at Sarain as she stared at her long lost friend, and knew by the look in her eyes that he no longer had her; once again she had slipped from his grasp, and this time she would be much harder to hold on to.

After a few hours of reminiscing it had grown very late in the night, and Orran rose from his seat saying, "It's getting pretty late, I should be heading out." "Are you sure?" Sarain quickly asked, "Where are you staying?" "The Scarlet Motel," he answered, and Sarain immediately said, "Oh that place is horrible. You should stay here."

Winston's eyes immediately bulged as he heard Sarain make the offer, but to hide his jealousy he did not protest. To his relief, Orran responded, "No I don't want

to impose, my room is fine. In fact, I've stayed in worse."
But Sarain pressed on by asking, "Well how about you
stay tonight. It's late and dangerous out there." Orran
chuckled as he remarked, "Hey, I used to train you, you
know I can take care of myself," then he gazed down at
Sarain and saw the almost pleading look in her eyes, and
said, "Fine, but just for tonight."

"Good, you can sleep in my bed," Sarain blurted
out, and then blushed when she realized how it sounded,
and quickly explained, "I'll take the den with Winston
here." "No, I don't want to put you out, I'll take the
floor," Orran relayed. "Well, there's more room on the
floor of the bedroom for you to stretch out on, anyway,"
Sarain commented. "Sounds good," Orran stated, and
Sarain showed him to the room.

Winston stood there feeling completely ignored
and neglected as he swallowed down the growing anger
of the thought of Orran being alone with Sarain in his
own bedroom.

Meanwhile, Sarain handed Orran a blanket and an
extra pillow for him to use. He laid them out on the floor,
and made himself a bed. Sarain crawled into her own, and
covered herself with a sheet, then asked as Orran lay
down, "Are you sure that's going to be comfortable
enough for you?" "The floor is about as comfortable as
the beds we had back with the clan," he remarked.
"Seriously, those things always hurt my back," she
replied. "They made for a good posture, or at least that's
what the chief use to say," Orran then added, causing

Sarain to think of her grandfather for a moment before muttering, "That's right, he did say that."

Sarain settled back into her bed, letting her tiredness come over her, and as she found herself beginning to drift off to sleep, she muttered to Orran, "I'm glad you're not dead." He gave a light chuckle to the randomness and child-like tone of the comment, and then replied, "I'm glad you're not dead, too."

Little Sarain smiled up at her mother, her handmade flower crown falling apart in her hair. Ariana smiled sweetly at her daughter as she went back to playing and collecting flowers.

"Are you making another crown?" Ariana asked. Sarain shook her head making a few flowers tumble out as she replied, "Nope, now I'm making a bouquet."

"But princesses don't carry bouquets, they carry scepters," Ariana explained to her daughter, who had been playing princess for the last hour. "I'm not playing princess anymore," Sarain commented. "No, then what are you playing now?" Ariana asked.

Sarain skipped as she walked over to a particularly big flower and answered, "I'm playing wedding." Ariana smiled at the cuteness that was her daughter's innocence, and said, "You'd make a beautiful flower girl." Sarain gave her mother a quick pout as she stated, "No mama, I'm a bride!" "Oh sorry," Ariana replied with a chuckle.

Ariana watched as Sarain collected a large assortment of flowers to the point that her daughter could barely hold them. Sarain then turned to her mother and said, "Mama, I need some ribbon for my bouquet." Ariana smiled and responded, "I think I have some, I can go get it in a little while." "Okay," Sarain said with a smile, she then went back to picking flowers.

"So who are you marrying today," Ariana asked her daughter. "Orran," Sarain quickly answered. "Again?" Ariana remarked, "Didn't you guys play wedding last week?" "Yes, but I want to play it again," she replied. "Well, I think Orran is busy playing with the big kids," she told her daughter.

Sarain then looked up and searched the field for Orran. In the distance she saw him playing with other boys, all of them carrying sticks in their hands and swatting at each other like they were swords.

"Orran!" Sarain shouted suddenly dropping her bouquet, "I want to play swords too!" She ran off into his direction leaving her mother behind. Ariana watched as her daughter joined the boys, and before long, dirtied her dress with mud.

Ariana smiled and took a deep breath, taking in the clean mid day air. She then strained to get up, and quickly stopped in place as she began to feel dizzy. A wave of nausea hit her, and Ariana knew that soon she would no longer be able to hide her sickness from her daughter.

Ariana reached for the pendent dangling around her neck and clutched onto it as she prayed for strength. After a moment she let it go, and her ankh dangled once more. Ariana pulled herself up, and began to walk towards the playing children.

She watched as her daughter ran after Orran, and while looking at the small boy, Ariana thought to herself, "Please, take care of her."

Chapter 7

Sarain opened her violet eyes to a dark room; with a windowless house the place was usually dark, leaving Sarain unable to judge what time of day it was. She felt groggy as she sat up reaching for her watch; it was late morning. She began to lay back down when it suddenly hit her; Orran. Sarain shot up in bed and looked over at the floor, and saw that it was empty. The extra sheets and pillow were folded and stacked in the corner where they had been when Sarain had first arrived at Winston's place. There was no sign of Orran having been there.

Sarain's heart began to race, had she dreamt of her reunion with him? She got up out of bed and left the room, searching for her lost friend. The hallway was empty, and Winston slept soundly and alone in the den. She then looked to the door and wondered if Orran had left.

Yes, he had left, he had woken up and left for his hotel; Sarain told herself. Orran was real, he was alive and real. Sarain then reached for the door knob. She stopped and quickly glanced back at the sleeping Winston, then turned the knob and crept outside.

The daylight was bright and hurt Sarain's eyes as it flooded at her too soon after leaving the darkened dwelling. She stepped out into the sunlight, and her eyes immediately focused on a figure standing near the hillside; Orran.

His back was to her and he stared out into the desert landscape. Sarain began approaching him, and he turned around as she neared. The sunlight shined from behind him, and he cast a long shadow that helped block the sun from Sarain's eyes. Orran's long dark hair that he had kept in a ponytail the night before now blew freely in the wind, his tanned skin almost glowed in the sunlight, and as he stared down at her with his hazel eyes, Sarain thought, how beautiful he looked.

Sarain's own skin had grown pale over the years, her hair hung to her waist; long, pitch black, and flat. Her hair once resembled Orran's with the streaks of amber and brown going through it from years of the sun lightening its strands. Now, Sarain knew she looked very different, and she was surprised that Orran had recognized her at all. Only her violet eyes gave her away.

Sarain stepped up to Orran, who gave her a smile as she approached and asked him, "What are you doing out here?" He took in a deep breath and said, "Fresh air and sunlight…" he exhaled, and remarked, "Your friend keeps a dark and dank place."

"It's not that bad," she said, "It's solid enough, and the lack of entry points makes it safe." Orran shrugged and then commented, "Maybe, but all that candle light is no substitute for the real thing."

Sarain was quiet, and then she looked away from her friend and out into the empty desert field. Orran followed her gaze, and after a moment asked, "What are you thinking?" Sarain looked up at him and asked, "Do you want to go for a walk?"

"Sure," Orran answered and then added, "What about your friend? Do you think he might want to join us?" Sarain shook her head, "No, he's not much of a morning person."

Sarain and Orran walked into town, talking of old times. They passed stores, and a few people along the way, but neither was interested in anything else than what the other had to say.

When they came up on a park, Orran stopped in place, then turned to Sarain and said, "Do you remember that day we played in a park like this?" Sarain smiled and replied, "Yes... You pushed me on the swing, because we had never gotten to play in a park before." "Hadn't you just turned thirteen?" Orran asked. Sarain nodded and answered, "Yeah, it was right before... the clan..."

They were both silent for a moment, holding their heads down. Eventually Orran turned and gazed at the empty swing set and then glanced back at Sarain and asked, "Did you want to?" Sarain smiled again at Orran and replied, "Sure."

They both walked over to the two empty swings, and sat down upon them. Sarain slightly swung back and forth as her feet dragged lightly on the sand. She looked over at Orran, who was staring out in front of them, and then followed his gaze to a woman playing with her son on the teeter totter. The boy was no more than three, and giggled as he watched his mother struggle to stay on the toy. The woman was about their age, she looked lovely and well groomed; not like Sarain, who didn't like to primp or wear makeup, as she thought to herself.

For a moment Sarain thought Orran was watching the woman, but when she got up to fetch her son a juice box, and Orran's attention didn't divert, she realized that he was watching the boy.

"What are you thinking?" Sarain asked him. Orran sighed and then looked to Sarain as he said, "Have you ever thought about having kids?" The question caught her off guard, and she wasn't sure how to respond, but after a moment, she remarked, "I can't have kids." Orran gave her a curious stare as she continued to explain, "I found out a few years ago that my body isn't capable of carrying a child."

He lowered his gaze from her as he said, "I'm sorry." Sarain sighed, "It's okay, fact is with a life of hunting, having a child isn't really practical. I mean look at us, even with a whole clan to support and raise us, we still barely made it out alive. I couldn't imagine being enough to protect a child with the life we live."

"You're right… Still, I've always wondered what it would be like to have the whole family experience," Orran stated once again watching the boy. His gaze then settled on the ground as he said, "I guess since we lost everyone at such a young age, it's always made me want a family of my own again someday….. A child to care over… A wife to love…"

It went silent as Sarain realized that she herself had once longed for a family, but that it had been a dream she had given up on a long time ago. Her eyes settled on the boy as she watched his mother carrying him away; the woman carried the child even though he looked too big for her arms, and though the tired child looked at peace in her arms, the serene look on the mother's face showed that the embracing act was just as much for her as it was for the child.

And then almost out of nowhere, Sarain heard Orran ask, "Are you 'with' Winston?" Sarain didn't answer right away, and instead searched her feelings before finally saying, "No."

Sarain heard Orran muffle out a small sigh of relief.

Sarain and Orran lingered in the park a little while longer before Orran finally decided that he needed to get back to his room at the Scarlet Motel. Sarain stood up immediately and Orran smiled down at her saying, "I'll be back soon, I just want to gather my notes first so that we can go over our findings together. Maybe we can figure out what's going on here in this town by working together."

"Do you want me to go with you?" Sarain asked. "No, you should get back and check on your friend. I assume he was still sleeping when you left... If he woke, he might be worried," Orran remarked.

Orran started to leave when Sarain grabbed his hand, he turned around, and she quickly hugged him. He smiled and patted her on the back saying, "Don't worry, I'm coming back." She then let go and he gave her one last smile before turning around and making his way out of the park.

Sarain made the trek back to Winston's home, alone, and all the while thinking of how strange and amazing it was to have Orran back in her life. But a part of her felt guilty, she had told Orran that she wasn't with Winston, but there was definitely something between them. Perhaps it was something more than friendship, though, whatever it was, was unclear to Sarain. She knew what Winston wanted from her, but now more than ever, Sarain was unsure if she could give that to him.

Sarain just hoped that Winston would give her the time and space she needed to search out her own feelings.

Sarain reached for the door to Winston's home, and cracked it open preparing to creep back in. Though as soon as she stepped inside the dark house, she was greeted with a displeased and almost frantic tone; "Where have you been?" Winston fretfully asked.

Sarain looked over to see Winston glaring at her as she simply answered, "I went out for a walk." "With him?" he quickly questioned. A puzzled and somewhat annoyed look came over Sarain's face as she replied, "Yes, I was with my old dear friend that I hadn't seen for seventeen years until last night."

Winston was quiet for a moment when he realized that he was sounding like a jealous spouse. He contemplated, and then said, "You could have at least told me that you were going out." "I didn't want to wake you, besides, I didn't think I'd be that long," Sarain remarked. Winston sighed, and asked trying to sound polite, "So did he leave?" "Yes, but he's coming back later," she answered to his dismay; Winston unable to hide his displeasure from his face.

Sarain rolled her eyes and turned away, stating, "He's bringing over his notes that he's made while hunting; he thinks they might be of some use to us." "Well, I guess that's good," he muttered.

Sarain then walked past Winston, and started heading down the hallway. He called after her, asking, "Where are you going now?" "To wash up, if that's okay with you?" she replied sarcastically.

Sarain entered the restroom, and quickly closed the door behind her, suddenly feeling crowded by Winston's insecurity. She lit a few candles for light, and then began to pump the handle for the water. Winston's house was old fashioned, and ran off of well water; Sarain was just glad that it had indoor plumbing. She pumped water about halfway full into the tub, and then stopped. She undressed and stepped into the cold water.

The chill didn't bother Sarain, she spent most of her childhood bathing in lakes and rivers, at least here she had privacy. She took a washrag and some soap, and lathered herself up. She made her skin look foaming, and she thought of how she used to play with the soap as a child; making herself look like a snowman.

Sarain rinsed the soap off her skin, and then dunked her head underneath the water, soaking her hair. She laid there for a moment, holding her breath, and listening to the sounds of the water splashing back and forth in the tub. Sarain thought of her life, and how complicated it had become. She was going through so many changes, that she barely recognized herself anymore, and now with Orran walking back into her life, Sarain was suddenly reminded of who she once was and how different she had become. She wasn't sure if he had noticed that the girl he had known was gone, but she knew that it was only a matter of time before he would see her for what she truly was; inhuman.

Sarain then realized that she felt scared; she didn't want Orran to see the demon side of her, she just wanted to be the girl that always made him smile. She felt a tinge of panic in her chest, and then a burning sensation.

Wait, it wasn't panic she was feeling, but pain. "Breathe", a voice inside of her said. And Sarain shot up in the tub, and took a deep and heavy gasp. She had held herself under all the while reflecting on her thoughts; she had forgotten to breathe.

Sarain quickly unblocked the drain, letting the water run out, as she clung to the side of the tub wondering, "How long was I without air?" Her wet hair dripped down her back sending a chill throughout her spine, as she realized just how long she had been under.

A tear rolled down her cheek.

Chapter 8

Sarain rang her hair out with the water raining into the tub. She wrapped a towel around her body, and opened the bathroom door to see Winston standing on the other side. She gave him a puzzled look, and asked, "Did you need something?" He stared at her for a moment, and it made Sarain uncomfortable, then he finally answered by saying, "No, I was just waiting on you."

"Okay…" she said still uneasy with his presence, and then went to turn toward the bedroom when Winston suddenly blocked her way. "Excuse me," she stated with annoyance, "I have to get dressed now." "Wait a sec," Winston quickly said, "I want to talk to you." "I'm sure it can wait," Sarain remarked clinging to her towel, making sure it stayed on, as she once again tried to pass him.

Winston then grabbed Sarain lightly by the arm, as he said, "But we still need to finish our conversation from yesterday." Sarain yanked her arm out from his grasp, "It can wait!" She hurried into the bedroom, and slammed the door close behind her.

Sarain quickly dressed, and then sat on the bed, thinking how she wasn't ready to have the conversation with Winston that he wanted, and his insistent behavior only pushed her further away.

She grabbed the towel and began drying off her hair as she thought of ways to divert from talking about the subject of "us" with Winston. Then a knock came at the bedroom door. Sarain sighed and got up, and opened the door to see Winston waiting impatiently. He looked helpless as he stared over at Sarain.

"You're pulling away from me, aren't you?" he asked weakly. Sarain hesitated to answer, not sure of what to say. She took a deep breath and looked Winston in the eye as she answered, "I need more time." He sighed then asked, "Is it because of him?" "Winston, please," she started to say, but then stopped when she noticed him beginning to lean in. Sarain's eyes avoided Winston's gaze as he lowered his face down to hers. She felt his cold breath against her skin, but just as his lips neared hers, a knock came to the front door. Winston hesitated from surprise, but Sarain didn't; with that cue she quickly slipped out from his approach, and headed for the door.

Her hand went to the cold metal knob of the door, and for a moment she felt a strange hesitation, like she had just done something wrong. She opened the door to see Orran standing there with his notes and a smile. Sarain then glanced at Winston, preparing to tell him of Orran's arrival, but when she saw the hurt look on his face, she knew he had already guessed who was visiting.

There was sadness, heavy in Winston's eyes, right before he looked away from Sarain, and she knew that once again she was hurting him.

Orran laid out his notes on the table while Sarain retrieved the hunter's journal she carried with her. When she handed it to Orran, she explained how she had found it, and then he proceeded to look through it as she glanced over his notes.

Orran kept detailed loggings of different places he had visited, creatures he had come across and killed, and folklore he had heard. As Sarain read through, and reached his more recent findings, she noticed him mention hearing of a group called "The Brotherhood".

"The Brotherhood?" Sarain said aloud. Orran looked up at her, and remarked, "It's why I came to this town." "The Brotherhood of Blood?" she asked. "Yes, they're supposedly the most dangerous demonic group known to man, and it's believed that they reside somewhere in this town," he explained. "They are here... I've already had a little run in with one of their members," Sarain stated. Orran gave her a wide-eyed stare as he said, "Really? What did it look like?" "He had wings," she replied.

Sarain watched as a look of recognition came over Orran's face as he muttered, "Kayne." Sarain gazed at him with puzzlement as he stated, "It's the beast's name; I've hunted him before. He's a nasty creature that leaves a trail of carnage just for sport, and not to feed. Apparently, he's very old and was made by some kind of greater eviler being, and that's why he has wings, though I can't imagine a creature nastier than him." "And you've hunted him before with no success?" Sarain asked.

"A demon that flies is not really the norm; he's taken out some colleagues of mine," Orran remarked a little defensively, and then asked, "How did you manage to get away?" "Just barely actually, it knew I was a hunter, it attacked, and Winston showed up just in time," Sarain replied. Orran gazed over at Winston who stood leaning against the wall a bit away from them, and then said, "Sounds like you're a good man to have in a tight spot." Winston glanced up for a moment and stated rather coldly, "I'd never let anything hurt Sarain."

Orran stared at him for a moment, noting Winston's hostility, but then turned his attention back to Sarain as he asked, "So you're hunting the Brotherhood too; have you located their hideout?" She shook her head and answered, "No." Orran then glanced at the hunter's journal and remarked, "You haven't even gotten any leads off of this passage?" "What?" Sarain asked, unfamiliar with his reference, and he handed her the book pointing to a particular entry that stated: They gather beneath his wings in his natural home, made unnaturally, and the beast rules over them like a god over men.

"Sure sounds like Kayne, doesn't it?" Orran commented. Sarain stared at the entry in amazement, but then mumbled, "Yeah, except he's not their leader." "What?" Orran quickly asked with confusion. Sarain then realized that Orran knew nothing of her father, but before she could respond, Winston quickly chimed in, "Well if this Kayne was supposedly made by something darker, then the obvious guess is he's not the one running the show." "Yeah, but that could be a myth, he could just be so old that he's evolved," Orran replied. "If he has been seen by as many hunters as it sounds like he's been, then he's not the big boss, but more like his lackey. The real leader would do a better job of staying hidden," Winston pressed, and Sarain immediately agreed with him by saying, "He's right. With how deadly and impervious this Brotherhood is suppose to be, their leader wouldn't have been spotted so much by people, and able to be described in this hunter's journal."

"Perhaps you're right," Orran remarked, "But the description of their hideout could still be valid; 'his natural home, made unnaturally'." Winston contemplated for a moment before saying, "There is an old abandoned mining cavern on the outskirts of town." Sarain glanced over at him as he explained his conclusion, "Well Kayne is bat-like, and a bat's natural home is a cave, but this mine shaft is man-made, hence 'his natural home, made unnaturally'."

"Sounds like a logical guess to me; it's worth checking out," Orran stated and then asked, "When did you want to check it out?" "Right after nightfall," Sarain remarked, and Orran gave her a funny look, so she explained, "They won't expect to be infiltrated on their own time and playing ground." It was a reasonable idea, but her real reason for the timing was so that Winston could come along.

Orran nodded an okay to Sarain, and then stated, "Well then I better go get my weapons; I didn't prepare for this big of a hunt." Sarain showed Orran to the door, and after she let him out and closed the door behind him, she turned to Winston, and said, "Thanks for covering for me back there." He glanced at her for a moment then replied, "I wasn't lying when I said that I'd never let anything hurt you."

Winston then left the room without another word.

Chapter 9

Sarain waited about an hour later in the den for Orran to return and Winston to retrieve his maps from deep in his closet. A knock came to the door first, and Sarain let Orran in. With him he carried a sword in hand, a machete strapped to his waist and a dagger in his boot. Sarain had her own sword and knife ready, and now they waited on Winston.

"Does he always run this late?" Orran remarked. Sarain glance over at him and replied, "I'm not sure, it's been a while since we've hunted together." "Oh," Orran muttered almost to himself as if making some kind of mental note, and then he asked, "How did the two of you meet?"

Sarain thought for a moment how to respond before answering, "We met on a job ten years ago; it was when I killed that demonic vil sang from the clan attack." "That couldn't have been easy," Orran commented, "He must be a good fighter, Winston that is." "He's one of the best I've worked with," she said.

Suddenly, Winston emerged with maps in hand, saying, "I've pinpointed the location of the mine." Orran stood up saying, "Are we ready to go then?" "I guess so," Sarain said, also rising from her seat.

Orran was out the door first, then Sarain with Winston following close behind her. She felt his hand brush her arm and she quickly glanced back at Winston, who whispered to her, "Did you really mean what you said back there? Am I really 'one of the best' you've worked with?" "Of course, I wouldn't lie about something like that," she answered, and then turned back around before seeing the smile form on his face.

The maps Winston brought showed the group that the old mine shaft was located in a mountain side, and when they reached the base of the mountain side, they saw that it was going to be quite a rough trek up.

Orran went first, he looked for knotholes in the rocky terrain that would make good footholds, and used the thick protruding rock side as gripping points for his hands. It took a lot of upper body strength for each person to pull one's self up the rock side, but as they got higher the mountain side began to level off.

"How exactly did the miners get to this mine?" Sarain called out to Winston. "There used to be a road, but there apparently was a nasty mountain slide many years back that destroyed it," he replied, "That's what closed down the mine."

The mountain side became more of a hike. No longer climbing, the three continued to travel up the mountain. The mine entrance came into view, but before they could reach it, they noticed a large stone step right before it. There were no knotholes to climb it, and the ground beneath it didn't look safe or stable enough to try and boost one another up. But before Sarain could suggest a plan, Orran leapt up, his arms grasping the top of the stone, and with a groan he pulled himself up.

Sarain's eyes were wide with amazement, it was quite a leap Orran had just made, she herself was unsure if she could do it. She looked up at him now crouching down on the stone above, extending his hand, and saying, "Come on, Sarain, I'll pull you up." Sarain grabbed his hand, and with him pulling, she used her legs to try and climb up the stone. It all happened so swiftly, that neither was sure of who did most of the work, but Sarain was now up on the stone.

Orran then quickly began to crouch down again to lower his hand to Winston, but before he could fully get into position, Winston had leapt for the stone like Orran had done before, ignoring Orran's offer to aide him. Except Winston's grip on the stone was poor, and he suddenly realized that he didn't have enough leverage to pull himself up. He began to slip, and before Sarain knew what she was doing, she grabbed Winston by the arm and yanked him up. She then turned to Orran who stared at her curiously; she had let her true strength show instead of letting him help, and she quickly stated in her own defense, "Must be adrenaline."

Orran then turned and headed for the mine, and as Winston stood there dusting himself off, Sarain muttered to him, "Quit being so stubborn." Winston glanced at her, as she continued saying, "You should have just let him help you." Then Sarain left to head for the mine shaft before he could thank her for helping him up in the first place.

The moonlight lit the entrance to the mine, but that was all. The mine was darker the deeper it went. Orran pulled out a lighter instead of a flashlight; he worried anything brighter would alert the demons of their presence, though Sarain knew that neither she nor Winston needed the aid of a light.

They walked as softly as possible through the dank cavern, looking for signs that demons were dwelling there. Everything appeared normal, the tunnels looked untouched. Orran continued to lead the way down the tunnel until they came to a dead end. He stared at it confused; there had been no other turn.

Orran then turned to Winston, and said, "Perhaps you were wrong about your guess of the creature's home." Winston shot him a dirty look as though his masculinity were in question, and then quickly grabbed the lighter out of Orran's hand and threw it at the rock wall. They all watched as the flaming lighter went through the wall as though it were air, and then Winston glanced over at Orran as he spoke, "This is definitely his lair."

With that, Winston took the lead, stepping through the mystical false wall. Orran picked up his lighter on the way, and relit it, then stared forward toward Winston with an odd expression on his face. Sarain noticed the look, and wondered if Orran was wondering why Winston had no trouble seeing in the dark.

They continued to walk on until lit torches came into view; they lined both sides of the tunnel and the ground turned into steps. Winston glanced back at Sarain and muttered, "Having any creepy flashbacks yet?" "A little," she whispered back, Orran all the while watching the two, curious of the reference.

They proceeded down the steps slowly, listening for sounds of movement or voices. As they spiraled down the stairwell, noises became apparent, and one side of the wall opened up. There was no railing and it looked to be a long drop down, so they stepped more cautiously. Sarain wondered what waited down below, and memories of the Purge and Sephor's army came flooding back into her head. And she remembered how Sephor had wanted her to lead his army.

The further down they went the more the crowd below came into view. A horde of demons of many kinds stared forward at a stage where Kayne stood, and Sarain hoped that perhaps he was their leader after all. After a moment he started to speak and the demons went quiet. He spoke, "A time of change has finally come; the Brotherhood's power is growing, and soon we will no longer be forced underground, we will walk amongst the prey above."

Sarain glanced at Orran, who looked at her with concern, both thinking of the raid on their clan. Kayne then continued speaking, saying, "There is a vision we have been seeking, a dream of one day walking in a sun that doesn't burn us. Not to be restricted to the shadows, but to rule over the cattle like the great beings we are." It sounded absurd to Sarain, the idea of demons walking in daylight, and then she thought of herself, and her father; both carrying demon blood and both capable of walking in sunlight. She continued to watch as Kayne rallied the crowd wondering if he was really capable of achieving the dream he preached, all the while having her doubts of it, until she heard him say, "And we will follow Father, and do all that he asks of us."

Sarain's heart began to race as she noticed Kayne cue to a form that suddenly teleported onto the stage, and she heard Orran whisper, "Is that a man?" Then she heard herself answer, "No it isn't," and she placed her hand on Winston's, causing him to glance over at her. Their eyes met and he knew immediately what she was trying to tell him; the creature that had just appeared on stage was no man, it was her father.

Chapter 10

Aion stood there, the crowd of demons in awe of him, and he looked exactly as Sarain remembered him. He still looked just like a man, his skin even slightly tanned, but Sarain could see the beast that she knew lurked inside. He waved Kayne back, and announced, "My children, as my powers continue to grow, a new hope emerges for achieving our dream; a child, born of my own blood, and capable of walking next to me in the sun. A new generation of power growing to help lead you all out of the shadows with me."

Sarain glanced at Orran watching his expression as he curiously listened on, and she wondered if he suspected her of being the child Aion spoke of. She was grateful that they were too far away for Orran to see the color of Aion's eyes.

"But your child kills our kind!" a creature called out, and within moments the beast was set aflame. "I will kill our kind if you have the nerve to doubt me!" Aion shouted. Sarain trembled as she realized just how powerful he was; she didn't know he could make someone combust instantly. Aion spoke again, "This child's will is not out of my grasp, and if you have doubts, there is another ready to lead my army. He is a great achievement of evolution, and another perfect example of what the power of my blood can achieve." Orran quickly glanced at Sarain and mouthed, "Kayne," and she knew that if she wanted to stop the Brotherhood she would have to take out both of its figureheads: Kayne and her father.

Sarain could feel fear building up inside of her, and she worried that she wouldn't be strong enough to take on Aion. Then she heard the raspy voice of Kayne shout in the distance, "Someone is on the staircase!" Winston suddenly grabbed Sarain and covered her eyes, and whispered in her ear, "I don't think he saw." She knew he wasn't talking about Kayne, but about Orran. She hadn't realized at the time that with all her growing fears, they had begun to show in the glowing of her eyes.

The group quickly turned to run, and Sarain heard to her relief Orran say, "How did they know we were here?" As they raced up the stairs, the horde of demons began to ascend at the bottom of the staircase. None saw as Kayne outstretched his wings and took flight after them, and Sarain certainly didn't see the smile that spread across her father's face. "Soon, my child," Aion muttered to himself.

Winston ran clinging onto Sarain's hand, making sure she didn't fall behind. They raced, passing the point where the wall came back to the other side of the staircase. Orran was a few steps behind them, and Sarain heard him shout, "Kayne is nearing!" She glanced over her shoulder to see Orran unsheathing his sword as Kayne flew towards him. Sarain then turned and shouted at Winston, who continued to pull her, "We have to help him!" But Winston didn't comply, and continued to drag her forward. Sarain stopped in her tracks, and suddenly yanked her hand away from Winston, then turned and raced toward Orran, grabbing for her sword.

Orran swung at Kayne, and his blade grazed the beast's wing. Kayne roared and detracted his claws and leapt onto Orran. "Orran!" Sarain shouted with fear in her voice, and she quickly raced at Kayne, and drove her sword partially into his back. It went in at an angle, with the blade going straight through, diagonally, catching mostly just flesh. Kayne twisted in agony and the blade came ripping out. He grabbed Sarain and threw her back against the wall, her back slamming against it hard enough to knock the wind out of her. He then raised one of his clawed hands to swat at her, when suddenly Winston threw himself at Kayne, knocking him away from Sarain.

The two tumbled down the staircase, and Sarain heard Winston shout, "Get her out of here!" The next thing she knew she felt Orran lifting her up and helping her run. She struggled to catch her breath, all the while trying to call out to Winston, who had fallen somewhere behind. They raced down the tunnel with the sounds of the horde of demons echoing from behind them.

The torches stopped, and then they ran through the darkness until finally they burst into the moonlight

and the coolness of the night air. Orran helped Sarain
down the rock side, as both stumbled to find good
footing. They raced down the mountain side expecting
for demons to burst out the mine's entrance, but they
never did.

Sarain worried that they had caught Winston, but
kept her fear buried down so not to let it show in her
eyes. She and Orran continued to run until they finally
reached Winston's home, and then both nearly collapsed
through the door.

They staggered inside, and then quickly closed the
door behind them. Sarain looked to Orran as she asked,
"Do you think the demons are coming?" "I didn't see
them leave the mine; maybe they didn't consider us as
much of a threat," Orran replied. Sarain thought to herself
how strange that was, and then she wondered if Aion had
told them not to chase after her, and realized that that idea
was much more logical, though she couldn't share it with
Orran.

She then glanced at Orran again, and with a
concerned tone, asked, "Did you see if Winston fell off
the staircase?" Orran noticed the worry on her face, and
was careful how he responded when he said, "I saw him
knock back Kayne, but I didn't see what happened after
that…I wounded his wing, if Winston managed to throw
him off the staircase, then he stood a good chance of
getting out of there; we had a good lead on the rest of the
demons." "That's true," Sarain muttered, and then
remarked, "I got a decent slash into Kayne myself, and
perhaps it threw him off his game."

Sarain's eyes then went to Orran's side and she saw that his shirt was shredded and damp. "You're bleeding," she observed as she began reaching toward him. "It's just a scratch," he remarked as he felt his side. "Either way, you still need to clean it," Sarain stated, and she led him to the bedroom where she kept her bag. She reached into her bag and pulled out a bottle of antiseptic and some bandages.

Sarain then looked up at Orran, a little nervous, as she told him, "You need to take off your shirt." Orran groaned as he stretched his arms up and pulled the shirt off. Sarain's eyes immediately went to Orran's blood stained side; the blood was caked to the wound. Sarain quickly poured some of the antiseptic onto a piece of cloth, and then slowly brought it to Orran's side. He barely flinched, but the muscles in his abdomen tensed.

"Does it hurt?" Sarain asked. "No, it just kind of tickles," he replied. She wiped away the blood, and with a sigh of relief, she said, "It's not bad, you won't need stitches." "I told you it was just a scratch," Orran responded with a smirk on his face. Sarain looked at him rolling her eyes, and said, "You always act like mister tough guy. How can I take you seriously?"

Orran continued to smile as he commented, "It's not an act, haven't you learned by now that I'm invincible?" Sarain began to laugh, and when her eyes went down she noticed a large scar across Orran's chest. The smile quickly vanished off Sarain's face as she remembered how Orran got that scar. The slash flashed in Sarain's mind as she brought her hand up to the raised skin. Orran's eyes lowered down to Sarain as he watched her fingers caress the smooth skin of the scar he bore.

Orran trembled, Sarain quickly moved her hand away from him, and asked, "Did I hurt you?" "No, your hand is just cold," he explained. A look of discontent came over Sarain face, and Orran quickly added, "It's fine; it just caught me off guard." But it wasn't the fact that Sarain made Orran tremble that bothered her, it was the fact that she hadn't noticed that her body was cold. In fact, she felt fine for someone whose body was hovering at room temperature.

Sarain began to turn away from Orran when he suddenly grabbed a hold of her hand, saying, "If you're cold, then I'll just have to warm you up." He cupped her hand in his, and then brought it to his mouth and exhaled his warm breath onto her skin. Sarain began to let herself smile once more, and Orran quickly brought his hand up to Sarain's face and caressed her cheek. "You always had the sweetest smile," he told her in a soft tone. "You could always make me smile," she muttered staring up at Orran.

And then just like in many of Sarain's fantasies, Orran leaned down toward her, their eyes locking, and slowly pressed his lips against hers. The kiss was soft and lasted only for a moment. Orran then quickly pulled away, turning his face away from hers, and saying, "I'm sorry, I didn't mean to take advantage of your kindness. It's just... I've wanted to do that for a very long time."

Orran turned back to Sarain with a look of guilt in his eyes, and as he started to turn away again, Sarain raised her hand to his face, gently, to stop him. She made him look at her, she stared up into his eyes, and then she stretched up and kissed him again. Her lips moved with his, parting and closing, pressing against him until they both felt the hunger and passion growing between them. Orran began to wrap his arms around Sarain, pressing her closer to him. The skin of his chest felt hot, and it warmed Sarain's own. She felt his hands on her back, under her shirt, and she raised her arms up as he lifted the garment over her head. He let the shirt fall to the ground, and raised his hand up to Sarain's neck and brushed back her hair. Orran then leaned down and began kissing her neck, sending quivering throughout her body. Sarain closed her eyes and sighed softly.

Orran began leading Sarain over to the bed, neither noticing that they had left the door cracked open, and both too enthralled in each other to see the pair of vibrant blue eyes glowing with fury in the doorway.

Chapter 11

Orran laid Sarain down onto the bed, and began to climb up on top of her. She started to pull him down for another kiss when a loud crashing sound suddenly broke their attention from each other. Orran leapt off the bed, and his eyes immediately went to the ajar door. He looked to Sarain, who had noticed it too, and muttered, "Winston." Orran grabbed Sarain's shirt off the floor and tossed it to her, and she quickly put it on.

More crashing noises echoed down the hall as Orran and Sarain stepped out of the room. They hurried down the hallway and into the living room to see that the room was a wreck; broken glass was scattered on the floor, and a chair lay broken against a wall.

Sarain's eyes quickly located Winston standing in the far corner of the room. He looked paler than usual and his eyes glowed brightly with rage as he stared at them. He began to approach them, and Sarain soon realized that he was approaching Orran. She glanced over at Orran to see a look of loathing forming on his face as he realized what Winston was. Then he was hit with the revelation that this wasn't a new development, but that Winston had been a vil sang the whole time, and Sarain had been keeping it from him. She began to step in between them, but Orran gestured Sarain back, saying, "No, keep away."

Winston glared at Orran with hatred in his eyes for a moment, and then turned to Sarain, and said, "With everything we've been through together, you go and betray me in my own home!" Sarain tried to speak, but before she could she heard Orran say, "You don't own her! In all the time I've been with the two of you, I've never even seen you two behave as though you were together. Just because you may wish it, doesn't make it so!" Winston looked astonished as he shouted, "She'd be with me right now if you hadn't come along!" "But I am here, and she didn't choose you!" Orran yelled back.

Winston brought back his hand to strike Orran when Sarain suddenly grabbed his arm in mid swing and shouted, "Stop it!" Winston pulled his arm away from her in disgust, and backed away. He began to head for the door when he stopped and turned to Orran, and said, "You may have known her first, but I got there first."

Orran's eyes went wide as he realized what Winston was saying, and a look of rage came over his face. He suddenly leapt at Winston and tackled him to the ground. Orran punched him in the stomach before Winston could react, and Sarain saw him gag. Winston then swung at Orran and his fist collided with his face.

Sarain moved toward the men who wrestled with each other on the ground, punching one another, and knocking into furniture. She grabbed at Winston, and pulled him up by his shoulders, she then slammed him against the wall, cracking a few of its stones. "Stay away from him!" she yelled at him then she turned to Orran, and bent down to check on him. The side of his face was red, and his lip was split and bleeding.

Sarain helped Orran up, as Winston watched in anger. She brought him gently to his feet, and as she wiped away the blood from his mouth she heard the crashing sound of the door slamming behind her. She looked over her shoulder to see that Winston was gone. Sarain then turned back around to see a look of disappointment on Orran's face. Her eyes softened as she gazed at him and asked, "What is it?"

Orran stared at her in disbelief as he asked, "You let that thing touch you?" Sarain hesitated to speak, and just stood there gazing up at him. Orran closed his eyes and turned away from her; she didn't need to say anything, he knew the answer.

Sarain stood there in the wrecked den, alone. She didn't know what to do, and wasn't sure what exactly she had done wrong, but she felt guilty. Her eyes settled on the ground, and with nothing else to do, she began to clean up the mess that was made.

Orran left a short time after that, without another word said.

Sarain stepped outside and into oddly stale air. The sky loomed and was gray, and though the dark clouds moved in a hurry far above her head, the air on the ground stood still. The sun was blocked out from the sky, and it looked as though a storm was about to hit. For as far as the eye could see there was nothing but sand and stone; the horizon was void of life. Sarain took another step out into the terrain, but she didn't know where she was headed. Within moments she turned back for the house, but the house was no longer there; it had vanished and was replaced with an equally desolate land. Sarain realized that she had become lost, and everywhere she turned there was nothing to be found.

Suddenly a crackle called out from above, and Sarain looked to the sky. A drop of water came falling from the clouds and landed on Sarain's forehead, it ran down her face, and fell off her chin. As the water dropped to the ground, more came pouring from the sky. Sarain's hair matted to her face, her clothes clung to her skin; she was drenched from head to toe, and she hung her head in shame as she began to feel helpless and alone.

Water splashed on the ground at Sarain's feet, and soon she saw the blooming of life beneath her. For a moment she began to have hope, until she noticed that the plant was not flourishing green, but was gray and looked dead. The brittle, shriveled plant continued to grow, and as it did, its thorns became apparent as was the fact that it was reaching out for Sarain. The dead vine began to wrap around Sarain's leg, digging its thorns into her skin. Where the thorns pierced, she saw her skin turn scaly and gray. Sarain tried to pull off the vine, but it tightened its grip on her leg and continued to wrap around her.

It wrapped around her waist and held her in place as she tried to struggle away. Sarain screamed as her arms turned gray, and she felt her skin growing deathly cold. She fell to the ground as the vine wrapped around her shoulders. Her eyes burned as they searched the landscape for someone who could help her, but there was no one in sight. No one could hear Sarain, or would come running to her aide.

Just before the thorny vine dug into Sarain's lips, she managed to call out one name, and it echoed throughout the terrain, and as the deadly plant cocooned her, Sarain could still hear the name calling out, "Mom."

Sarain shot up in her sweat drenched bed, struggling with the sheets. She fell off the bed and came crashing to the ground with a loud thud. Her eyes glowed as she ripped the sheets off of her. Once she realized that she had woken from her dream, she tried to catch her breath, and make herself calm, but before she could, she heard a cruel chuckle come from the doorway.

Sarain looked up to see Winston staring down at her, "Did you win the battle?" he asked in a crude tone. His expression looked cold, and for a moment, Sarain remembered seeing a similar look in his eyes when she had first met him at the Purge.

Sarain groaned as she straightened up and then replied in her defense, "What are you even doing here?" "It's my house," he quickly answered. "No, here in this room," she stated. "You were crying out for your mommy," he remarked rudely. Sarain stood up and returned the sheets back onto the bed as she muttered, "And what part of that sounded like your name?"

Sarain then glanced over at Winston who looked angry. He stated, "Whatever, I'm only here to get my things." "You're leaving?" she asked, a bit surprised. "I'm going to go stay at Julianne's until you are done with whatever you needed to do out here," Winston responded, grabbing some clothes out of his dresser.

Sarain was shocked to hear that Winston was back with Julianne, but then quickly remembered the lifestyle he had lived when she had met him, and then was not surprised that he couldn't be alone. She did ask, "So you're not going to help me?" "Why? You don't need my help, you have Orran... that is, if you haven't chased him away yet," he replied smugly. "Lucky for me, he doesn't scare easy," Sarain shot back. Winston looked over at Sarain as he remarked, "Perhaps if he knew the truth, he would." He then took his clothes and left the room.

Sarain was angry, but she knew what Winston had said was true; that if Orran knew the truth about her origin, he likely wouldn't look at her the same.

It was early evening; Sarain had slept the day away. She dressed and quickly left for the Scarlet Motel to see Orran. Winston had already taken what he needed, and was gone before Sarain left the house. She hiked the desert hillside with stars twinkling in the sky and the moon shining down on her. A cool breeze blew against Sarain, and the night felt peaceful. She made it to the hidden stairwell, and stepped inside its darkness. She made out the steps in the dark as she wound around the staircase.

Suddenly Sarain heard the echo of a step coming from above, and she quickly stood still to listen more closely. Another step followed, and soon Sarain saw the beam of a flashlight. As the person turned the corner and approached Sarain, the flashlight's beam quickly settled on her.

"Oh," she heard the person say, as they lowered the light. Immediately her eyes adjusted and she recognized Orran standing in front of her. "What are you doing here?" she asked. "I was coming to see you," he answered, and then with a curious look, asked, "How can you see anything in this darkness?" "Spend enough time hunting creatures in it, and your eyes will adjust too," Sarain quickly replied, and then added, "Besides, anything that I'd have to worry about will have glowing eyes." "True," Orran stated, he then gave a quick glance around, and said, "Let's move out of here." Sarain nodded and followed Orran back out of where she had just come from.

They stepped out into the desert terrain. Sarain looked up at the sky for a moment before finally asking Orran, "So were you coming to talk about last night?" He nodded, and muttered, "A lot happened yesterday. It's probably better if we talk about it, instead of just trying to ignore it." Sarain agreed, but felt a tinge of fear over what Orran might say, or think of her now.

He cleared his throat before saying, "So I understand why you hid the fact that Winston is a vil sang from me. I don't like nor trust what he is, and I know you would know that about me, but I don't understand why you hid the fact that you had a relationship with him, even when I thought he was human." Sarain took a deep breath before answering, "The truth is, I was only with Winston once, ten years ago, and we only recently met up again, and became friends... I know I probably should have told you anyway, but with everything going on..." And Sarain stopped, she looked away and was quiet for a moment, until finally she gazed back at Orran and said, "Look, I'm not the same girl you once knew; I've been through a lot of hard times, and for the most part, I've done it alone. I can't change what I've done, or who I am, and if you can't accept that, then there's nothing else I can do."

Orran gave her a contemplative look, and then asked, "How well do you know Winston?" "He's saved my life multiple times, and has helped me fight his own kind; that's all I really need to know," she quickly replied. "Okay, I understand your caution; you've spent a lot of time having to protect yourself, I can't expect our knowing each other as kids to make me an exception," Orran remarked. Sarain felt a slight tinge when she heard what Orran had said, that's not how she felt about him at all, but her need to protect herself was truly causing her to hold back.

"Orran…" she started to say, but he stopped her by saying, "No, it's okay, I don't blame you. I just saw the girl I once knew, and wanted to jump right back to how we were as kids, I didn't stop to think that maybe that wasn't how you felt." Sarain let out a soft sigh, but Orran didn't notice it, and continued to say, "I just wanted to protect you and be there for you like after your mother died, and you were stuck alone with your grandfather. I guess it didn't dawn on me that you had learned to take care of yourself, and didn't need me anymore."

"Orran, it's not like that," Sarain suddenly interrupted him, "I learned to take care of myself, because I had to, it wasn't because I preferred it that way. Maybe that's how it became later on, but that's only because I had lost so many people dear to me, that I was afraid of it happening all over again… Orran, I never forgot you, in fact, a few days after the clan attack, I went back to our camp to retrieve a few things, one of which was a photo of us, that I still carry around with me to this day."

A look of surprise formed on his face. "If you came back to the camp, why didn't you look for me?" Orran asked stunned by what Sarain had just relayed. "I thought you were dead, all the bodies were gone, and someone had dug graves. I figured yours was one of them," she replied. "But you didn't stick around?" he said, slightly questioning her. "Some people I didn't recognize chased me off; you know we were taught not to trust outsiders, and I didn't know if they were looters, criminals or what," she explained.

Orran quickly raised his hand to his forehead and groaned, and then he remarked, "The day I was well enough to go back to the camp, the hunters that found me said that a looter had taken some unknown items from one of the dwellings, but that they were unable to catch the thief."

Sarain let out a gasp when she realized what Orran had already figured out; they had just barely missed each other that day, many years ago. "Oh god," she muttered, as a tear escaped her eye. She looked up at Orran, and started to tell him that she was sorry, but before she could get the words out, he quickly took a hold of her, and kissed her on the lips.

Orran held her tight there under the moonlight, and as he did, he whispered to her, "It's okay, we found each other now."

Chapter 12

Orran and Sarain sat on the hill side under the light of the moon. Sarain looked up at the stars while Orran looked at her. Sarain, sensing his stare, turned to Orran and asked, "Did we run out of things to talk about already?"

"Actually, I was just thinking about the other night while we were spying on the brotherhood," he replied. "Oh," she asked curiously, "What were you thinking?" "Well, taking out the whole army won't be an easy task, but Kayne does often hunt separately from the group. If we can lure him away, then perhaps we can take him out together," he explained. "But what about the rest of the brotherhood?" Sarain questioned.

"Well if Kayne is their leader's enforcer, he should be weakened without him," Orran stated. Sarain gazed at him, knowing that his plan was flawed as she said, "We don't know how strong this leader is, killing Kayne might not affect him at all." "A demon is still a demon, they all have a weakness," he remarked. "Not this demon," Sarain muttered, and then Orran turned and glanced at her curiously. "Do you know something I don't?" he asked her. Sarain searched the night sky with her eyes, and answered, "You don't get to be the leader of a demon army, and have the ability to set fire to beasts with your mind or to teleport when you have weaknesses. And those are only just the things we've seen him do, who knows what else he's capable of."

"Perhaps you're right, maybe we are looking at a new breed of demon altogether, but I am curious of something," Orran remarked. "What?" Sarain asked. "The leader spoke of an heir, one that kills its own kind," he said, and Sarain quickly stated, "How's that of any use if we don't know what or where it is? With all the demons out there, the heir could look like anything." "Still, if we could get it to work with us, such an ally could prove useful," Orran remarked. Sarain glanced at him again, and said, "I thought you didn't trust demon blood." "I thought you believed that some of them could be trusted?" he responded while looking back at her.

Sarain let her gaze fall to the ground, and then quickly changed the subject by saying, "Maybe we should get in a hunt tonight, you know, stop talking and get into action?" Orran gazed over at Sarain and with a smirk said, "I've been wondering if you'd be able to keep up with me."

She gave him a slight smile and stated, "I think I'll do okay."

They wandered the dark deserted streets, walking alley after alley. It was a small town, causing them to retread the same streets again and again. Sarain wondered how the whole brotherhood army survived on such a small town, and with hardly any news of missing or murdered people. Surely the demons had to feed, Sarain was just curious to what their source of nourishment was. With her father being in charge, just about anything was possible.

As the hours went by it began to look as though the hunt would be uneventful. Orran turned to Sarain and muttered, "Did you want to call it quits for tonight?" Sarain continued to walk a few paces then stopped; she turned to Orran, and raised a single finger to her lips signaling for him to be quiet.

A moment earlier, Sarain had heard what sounded like an extra set of footsteps trying to match up with their own; it almost sounded like their footsteps were echoing in the distance, but Sarain knew that that was impossible with this kind of terrain. Her eyes scanned the area looking for places in which a pursuer could hide. Down the alley behind them stood empty, but Sarain was sure the source of the sound had to be down that way. She began to double back in search of a stalker when suddenly Sarain heard Orran whisper her name. She turned back around, towards him, and he nodded towards some bushes off in the distance that were moving against the breeze.

Sarain gave a puzzled look, wondering how the pursuer managed to double around so quickly and without being noticed. She slowly stepped to Orran and together they approached the bushes, and just as they neared, the branches began to shake violently. A loud snap echoed out followed by a large demon leaping out towards them. It lunged at Sarain, as though it were assuming she'd be easy prey due to her size. And she quickly leapt up into the air with the beast passing underneath her.

Orran seemed impressed, but his attention was quickly turned when he saw the two other demons following the first one out from their wooded hiding place. He withdrew his sword as one of the demons began to charge at him; he turned and swung as the beast leapt by, cutting it across its side. It crashed to the ground and struggled to get back up. The other beast quickly lunged at Orran, knocking the sword out of his hand, and sending him crashing to the ground.

Sarain glanced over as Orran struggled on the ground with the beast, and made motion to help him, but before she could the original demon grabbed at her and pulled her towards itself. The beast got a hold of her ankh by mistake, and it wailed as it burned the creature's flesh. It jerked and broke the cord off Sarain's neck, and then grabbed at her again growling and snarling its teeth at her as it drooled from its mouth. Sarain heard Orran groan during his struggle, and as a reflex, she grabbed at the beast's throat and ripped it out. The demon collapsed dead to the ground, but Sarain quickly swung her blade at it and behead the creature; she didn't want Orran asking questions of how she had killed the thing.

Sarain then turned back to Orran just in time to see him kick the demon off of him. He struck the creature with both his feet sending it flying back into the air. Sarain was a little surprised knowing how heavy a demon of that size could be. She saw Orran start to reach for his sword, when the beast began to charge again.

"Orran!" she yelled out, and his eyes shot forward. He left the sword on the ground, but instead of dodging the demon, he braced himself and grabbed a hold of its head as it tried to ram him. The demon had bull like horns protruding from its skull that Orran now gripped a hold of. He held tightly onto its horns, and Sarain expected to see the demon shake him off, or even send him flying, but Orran barely even budged as the demon struggled. Sarain watched as Orran shifted his grip on the horns, and then suddenly twisted the demon's head causing a loud and sickening snap. The beast fell limp to the ground, and Orran reached down and picked up his sword.

Sarain stared at him in disbelief, realizing that Orran was stronger than she had estimated; she had never seen another hunter pull off the kind of feats that only she had done before. She started to walk towards him, when she saw Orran quickly raise his sword and throw it towards her. Sarain flinched and then heard a thud behind her; she turned around to see Orran's sword protruding from the neck of the beast he had wounded earlier.

She turned back around towards Orran, her eyes wide as she said, "Next time a little warning before you do that!" Orran smiled at her as he made his way to her and replied, "Sorry, I didn't have time." He then bent down and picked up Sarain's ankh from the ground, as he stated, "Here, I think your mom would want you to keep a better hold onto this." Orran then reached behind Sarain, and retied the ankh back onto her neck.

His fingers grazed her neck as he lowered his hands back down. The touch of his skin on hers sent a quiver throughout Sarain, and she quickly grabbed his hand and stared up at Orran. She stretched up and kissed him on the lips, and soon felt him kissing her back. The amazement that Orran was alive and now kissing her, still felt unreal to Sarain. After a moment Orran broke from the kiss and rested his forehead against Sarain's as he smiled and said, "You know, this really isn't the most romantic place for this."

Sarain glanced down at the dead demon bodies around them and then gave a light chuckle as she replied, "Perhaps you're right." "Come on, let me take you home. It's getting pretty late," he suggested.

Orran continued to hold onto Sarain's hand as they walked back to Winston's. The stars that had earlier sparkled above now began to fade with the approaching dawn, and the sky turned to shades of gray and blue. Nothing about Sarain's life ever felt normal, but as she walked hand in hand with Orran, for once she felt like a regular girl on a date with a boy she had a huge crush on.

As they arrived at their destination, Sarain felt a bit of disappointment with the realization that the night had truly ended. She turned and looked up at Orran who had the dawning sun shining behind him, and asked, "Did you want to come in?" Orran shook his head as he answered, "Not with Winston in there." "He's not staying here anymore," Sarain quickly stated, "He went to stay with an old girlfriend." "Wow, isn't he the dedicated one," Orran muttered sarcastically under his breath. "Come on, it's not like him and I even had anything going; he's free to do what he wants," Sarain replied.

"I don't know, the guy just gives me the creeps," Orran remarked. Sarain stared at him curiously, as he explained, "Well, you know I'm no fan of vil sangs, but besides that, here he's been living in the same town as the infamous Brotherhood of Blood, and they haven't killed or recruited him; I mean really? He was the one who found their lair, and knew their little glamour tricks. In fact his home is located in a nice and strangely hidden location from humans, and then he somehow manages to escape safely out of their lair the other night, all alone, and with a horde of demons chasing after us. You have to admit that that sounds a bit suspicious."

Sarain only thought it over for a second before shrugging and replying, "Yeah, a little bit, but Winston's not that guy anymore." "Anymore?" Orran quickly noted, "What's that suppose to mean?" Sarain realized her slip of the tongue, and stated, "Let's not worry about this right now; trust me, Winston's not a problem."

Orran groaned, and Sarain gazed up at him again, and asked, "So did you want to come in?" "No thanks, I'm in no hurry to spend time in the guy's house. You probably should find somewhere else to stay as well."

Sarain gave him a look, but didn't give him a response; she was disappointed in his actions. Sarain then stretched up to give Orran a kiss, but he moved away. She stared up at him in disbelief and disappointment, and Orran quickly caught the dismay in her eyes. He raised his hand to Sarain's face, and softly caressed her cheek, as he said, "You should get some rest. I'll be by here tomorrow."

Sarain nodded and forced a smile as Orran turned to leave. She then went inside, closing the heavy door behind her, and shutting out the light from the dark dwelling. She walked to her room, sat down on the edge of the bed, and began to think over what Orran had said; it was odd, all the circumstances that surrounded Winston. She wondered how he hadn't crossed paths with the brotherhood before, living in the same small town as their headquarters.

Sarain reminded herself that Winston had once worked for a similar organization before. Could she really trust that her brief influence on him ten years earlier could really have such a lasting effect on him to stop him from ever working with another evil demon army again? It's something he knew and did well; she could still hear Sephor's words burning in her ears about how Winston was the best in the business of luring victims in. Sarain knew Winston had no real reason to be loyal to her, both as a man and a demon, but a part of her didn't want him to be the bad guy. Something about the thought of one day fighting Winston didn't sit well in the pit of her stomach. Sarain wanted to sooner believe that Orran was being jealous and overly cautious; it was what a hunter did.

And then she remembered Eddie not trusting James in the same way, years earlier, and her not listening to him cost him his life. She couldn't let that happen to Orran, but she didn't want to hurt Winston either. Though she knew that she could no longer blindly trust him, she had to start keeping a watchful eye on Winston, if he bothered to come around again. Winston's sudden absence began to make Sarain doubt the devotion he claimed to have for her; his love and faith in her only extended to her if she was able to reciprocate those feelings, and that her mere friendship wouldn't be warranted.

Perhaps Winston wasn't the man Sarain wanted him to be, but still she prayed he wasn't the monster Orran suspected him of being.

Chapter 13

Sarain woke the next day during mid afternoon; she sat on the ground outside under the sun feeling its rays beating against her skin. This time of the year the weather should be a lot colder outside, but today it felt hot out as the sun caused Sarain to sweat.

She stared down at the photo in her hands, the one of her and Orran as kids. So much had happened since that day, and Sarain wondered if they were still anything like those kids in the picture; Orran seemed stronger, but still resembled that lighthearted boy. Sarain on the other hand felt as though she had grown cold and disconnected, she no longer held onto hope like the girl she once was. In fact, Orran was the only thing that brought any of the old Sarain out. Being with him made Sarain feel alive again and not so destined for cruelty; he was the only thing that felt like family to her.

Sarain sat there until the sun began to set, and as dusk started to set in, she heard the footsteps announcing Orran's arrival. She quickly tucked the photograph into a pocket on the side of her boot, and stood up to greet Orran.

"Sorry I didn't get here earlier," Orran stated. "It's okay," Sarain replied, "I do expect for you to take some time to sleep." She glanced at Orran curiously, noting that he was wearing a jacket, and asked, "Aren't you warm wearing that?" He looked at her with puzzlement as he answered, "No, it's cold out." Sarain glanced at Orran again, and felt conflicted with his response as a drop of sweat ran down her back, but she didn't mention it again.

"Anyway," Orran said with a hint of excitement in his voice, "I'm late, because I found evidence of a lair of demons in town." "The brotherhood?" Sarain asked. "No, I don't think so. They seem to be their own little pack; four or five of them. More like animals than an army," he answered, and then added, "I thought we could take them out together, tonight, before they move again." "Okay, but you seem a little eager to hunt," Sarain observed. "Do I?" he asked, and explained, "It must be the love of having another hunter to fight with." "It is different working with a partner who can take care of themselves," she remarked, "I'll go get my weapons."

Sarain hurried inside, and as she grabbed her sword, she was suddenly struck by an odd feeling; something felt out of place. She quickly glanced around the room, but everything appeared to be ordinary. She grabbed her sword and ignored the strange feeling as she went back to Orran outside. He immediately noticed the odd look on her face, and asked, "Is something wrong?" "I don't know," Sarain responded, "Something just doesn't feel right." "Are you feeling sick?" he questioned. "No….no, I'm sure it's nothing," Sarain said still trying to ignore her feelings. Orran gazed at her with concern in his eyes as he said, "Well let me know if you're not feeling well, we can do this another night." "No, I'm good... Let's go," Sarain assured him.

Orran took a step closer to Sarain, and then leaned down and kissed her on the forehead, and then he muttered, "I see you're still that kid trying to keep up with me." "I'm not a kid anymore," Sarain stated with a bit of tension in her voice. Orran glanced down at her, and then remarked, "I can see that." He then bent down and kissed her on the lips, and for a moment, Sarain almost forgot all about the demon lair they had planned to clear out. She kissed Orran back, pulling down on the collar of his jacket, until Orran finally broke away, panting a little. "You make it really hard to focus on the job at hand," he muttered, and Sarain gave him a smile.

"We should get going then," Sarain stated, and Orran led the way. They walked the desert landscape to the hidden staircase, and as they ascended the darkened passage, the feeling that something was off emerged in Sarain once again. The echo in the stairwell seemed strange to her, though their footsteps sounded normal, the wind moving through the passage did not. It sounded muffled, but Sarain knew she was no expert on the weather, and couldn't say for sure that something was wrong. Yet still she felt on edge.

They exited through the secret entrance, and now were in the busy alleyway market. Orran led Sarain past the booths and people, some of the while holding her hand, making sure not to lose her in the crowd. His hand was warm against her cold skin, but he didn't remark to it; Sarain figured that he would assume it was because of the cool night air and not something at fault with her.

Sarain kept her eyes down as they passed closely to the people, but when the breeze picked up, a gust of wind blew between them causing Sarain's hair to fly loose, she quickly glanced behind her to see where her hair tie had fallen and caught a glimpse of something that struck her with discomfort. She caught a sudden glimpse of a figure in a dark cloak, or at least so she thought. Within seconds the figure had vanished from her sight as though it was never there. She immediately thought of Kayne on her first night there, stalking her through the marketplace; was he following her again?

Orran continued to tug Sarain along, and she left the hair tie behind. As they neared the end of the marketplace, Sarain gave another glance over her shoulder to the alleyway behind them, but saw nothing suspicious. Orran let go of Sarain's hand as they walked down the vacant streets, it may have only been early evening, but the rest of the town seemed dead like it was in late hours.

When they walked through widely open streets, Sarain continued to glance behind her, but saw no one following them, and she began to think that her mind was playing tricks on her. She then looked to Orran and whispered, "How much further?" "Not long now," he muttered as he stared forward.

Another cool breeze blew through Sarain's hair, and she felt a chill go down her spine; something definitely didn't feel right about that night. She gazed forward at the back of Orran and wondered if she would be able to protect him from any unforeseen dangers ahead. Sarain placed a hand on the hilt of her sword to ensure her readiness.

They had now reached the industrial side of Shaven; where all its warehouses were kept. Orran then turned down another alleyway; it was narrow and dark, and at the end of it was a door. He glanced back at Sarain, and whispered, "They're in there." Sarain gazed at it curiously; the structure of the alleyway and the door seemed odd, and didn't make sense for a warehouse, even an old abandoned one, to be setup in such a way. There was no room for loading and unloading of merchandise, making Sarain wonder what the building had been originally used for.

Orran stepped softly towards the door, trying not to alert the inhabitants inside of their presence. As Sarain neared, she began to wonder how Orran had found out about such a lair, in all his excitement in relaying what he had found to her, he never actually told her how he had found the place. The door hung slightly ajar, but only darkness could be seen behind it. Orran pushed the door open without it making so much as a groan, and he carefully stepped inside the shadowy building. He held his hand out for Sarain, and as she began to take it, she suddenly heard a voice call out, "No! Don't go in there!"

It took Sarain a moment to realize that the voice was not in her head, but instead coming from the alleyway behind her. She quickly turned around to see a cloaked figure standing at the entrance of the alley. Her free hand tightened around her sword, but she hesitated to draw it when she saw the blue glow of eyes coming from within the hood of the cloak. The figure wasn't Kayne, it was Winston, she suddenly realized.

In that unexpected moment of confusion, Sarain stood in hesitation. She stared back at Winston, unsure of what was happening, but before she knew it, a hand gripped tightly around her wrist and tried to yank her inside of the dark warehouse. The sudden forceful tug shocked Sarain back into reality and she struggled to fight back. Her arm initially disappeared into the darkness and she realized that the building was not just shadowy, but was in fact made up of darkness; when her arm was inside it had disappeared from her view completely.

She fought to tug her arm back, but was surprised by the amount of force that was pulling her. Sarain yelled in frustration, and immediately felt a pair of arms wrapping around her waist and pulling her in the opposite direction; Winston was helping her tug back. Slowly, Sarain's arm began to reemerge from the darkness, and with one final forceful tug, her arm was free. Sarain and Winston fell back onto the pavement, and she heard a voice call out, "You can't protect her forever." It sent a quiver down her spine; it wasn't the voice of some dreadful demon, but instead of her beloved Orran.

The doorway immediately vanished like magic, and there was nothing there, but an old broken gutter barely hanging to the wall. Sarain panted heavily as panic began to set in, and she heard herself asking, "What was that?" "That was a portal hidden by a glamour," Winston answered. "But…Orran," Sarain started to stammer. "He shouldn't have even been able to see the door, if he had been human," Winston stated, before Sarain could finish.

She glanced up at him in shock as Winston began to stand up, and asked, "How is that even possible? Orran can walk in the daylight!" "Didn't you say your father could do the same thing?" he remarked. "But my father is an ancient, Orran…Orran is…" the words wouldn't come out. Winston then bent down and pulled Sarain up as he stated, "Orran is working for them."

Chapter 14

Winston took a distraught Sarain back to his home, she didn't say much on the way back or even put up a fight; she just followed him quietly gazing at the ground. When they arrived Winston took her straight to the bedroom where she sat down on the bed and stared blankly at the floor. Winston began to close the door to give Sarain her privacy when he heard her say, "How did you know Orran wasn't human?"

Winston hesitated for a moment before finally answering, "I didn't know before, I just didn't trust him." Sarain didn't respond, so once again Winston began to close the door, but stopped when she asked, "Were you following me this whole time?" He sighed, and just before he closed the door he muttered back, "Yes."

Winston walked down the hall, back to the den, and removed his heavy cloak. He placed it on a hook and hoped he wouldn't need it again for day time walking anytime soon. He then brushed off his dirty clothes and thought of taking a bath to wash off the filth of a few days of camping out in the wilderness. He glanced down the hallway and thought of Sarain. He wondered what was going through her mind at that very moment, and if telling her that he had never stayed at Julianne's would make a difference. He shook the thoughts out of his mind and he reminded himself that he was not her precious Orran, and that she alone had gotten herself into this mess. But as he started to gather clean clothes for a bath he paused and thought of Sarain's eyes; they had looked so vacant of emotion when he left her in the bedroom, at least in the past she would get sad or angry, but now, in her eyes, there was nothing there. The only place Winston had ever seen eyes so vacant before was in the broken victims that were turned into vil sangs back at the Purge those many years ago.

It was like she was void of hope.

Sarain watched as demons ripped through her clan's camp, setting fires to some of the dwellings, and murdering every man, woman, and child they came across along the way. She felt trapped inside her crate, unable to aide any of the friends she saw fall before her. She watched helplessly as Orran stepped up to the monster she would one day know as Sephor. The boy swung his sword at the beast and with a lucky hit struck it on its arm managing to break open its stone like flesh.

Sarain's heart held onto the hope that the outcome of the fight would end differently this time, but when she saw Sephor swing his sword at Orran, striking him across the chest, she heard the inevitable gasp she tried to hold in. Once again she saw Orran make the mistake of pausing to look towards her hiding spot giving Sephor the time to grab the boy, and sink his teeth into his neck.

Sarain felt her heart breaking once again as she watched the life draining from Orran's eyes. But as she waited to see her friend's body drop, she noticed a change in Sephor's movements. Instead of throwing the boy's body to the ground, he held him up against him, and with a quick motion, took his sword to his own wrist and slit it open. Black blood trickled out from his stone skin, as he brought his wrist to the boy's lips.

Sarain watched in horror as Sephor forced his blood into Orran's mouth, and began rattling in her crate, screaming, "No, this is not how it happened!" She saw the look in Orran's eyes begin to change, their once beautiful hazel color slowly began to change, and soon they became yellow like Sephor's. It was then that Sephor finally let the boy go, letting Orran collapse to the ground.

Sarain watched for a moment as Orran lay still, knowing that this wasn't right, the dream had changed. Orran was not going to get up; he wasn't supposed to move, but alas, she saw his body twitch, his arm shift, and his head began to rise. Slowly Orran began to raise himself up from the ground; he was covered in both human and demon blood. She saw the gaping wound on his neck still pouring out his blood, and watched as he raised his eyes up towards her crate. His eyes burned yellow, and Sarain realized in that moment the beast inside Orran knew that she was inside.

She watched as Orran crawled towards her, his face scowling like a rabid animal's. She struggled to break free of her crate, hoping to run from the frightening sight of her transformed friend. The crate's lid popped off and Sarain quickly struggled to climb out the box. As she swung one leg out, she felt someone grab hold of her hair and yank it. Her head snapped back, shooting pain throughout her neck, but nothing more than a bad case of whiplash. Orran stared down at her, her dark hair wrapped around his fist; his eyes blazed down at hers, and they held no love within them.

"Orran please!" she cried out. He hissed at the sound of her cry, peeling his lips back to expose his new fangs. Tears rolled down Sarain's cheeks as she yelled out again, this time saying, "You're not Orran!" It looked like her friend, but he had been replaced by a soulless beast. He then lowered his head down to her neck, and as he sank his teeth into her throat, Sarain heard her voice ringing out in her head, "My Orran is dead."

Suddenly Sarain shot up in bed, she was covered in sweat, but her body felt cold. It was just a dream, Sarain realized, but then she remembered the events of that night, and it occurred to her that the nightmare wasn't over. Her father and his demon army were still out there, and they had Orran.

"No, that wasn't Orran," Sarain muttered to herself, and then a voice came over from the doorway, saying, "I've never known demons to shape-shift. If a beast looks like someone and has all their memories, it generally means that they are that person."

Sarain turned towards the door and saw Winston standing in the doorway, watching her. She stared at him for a minute before she said, "Maybe he once was Orran, but if he's working for Aion, then he's not in there anymore." "That's not how it works; you should know better with your situation. The demon blood doesn't destroy the man, but instead brings all his flaws and hatred to the surface," Winston remarked, "Not all of us turn into mindless beasts. No, at some point we all have to make a choice… You have to choose to become evil, it doesn't happen overnight."

"So you're saying that Orran chose to be a monster?" Sarain asked, and then glared over at Winston as she suddenly changed subjects by saying, "Why are you even here?" "You were calling out 'his' name again," he stated angrily. "And why does that have anything to with you?" she responded back in frustration. Winston shook his head with aggravation, "That's it; it never has anything to do with me! Ever since I've known you, it's always been his name you call out; in your sleep, when you're hazy, and even when I save you. You never want it to be me; you always want it to be him. It doesn't matter if he's dead or a demon, you've only ever cared about Orran!"

"I'm too tired to deal with this now," Sarain groaned. "I don't care, you're going to listen to me now! I've done everything I could possibly do for you, so why is it that I can never measure up to the memory of that guy?" Winston pleaded. "Oh my god," Sarain muttered as she got up out of bed, "I'm not having this conversation." "Is my skin too cold, too pale, have I not killed enough demons for you?" he shouted.

Sarain grabbed her coat, and then pushed past Winston in the doorway. He grabbed a hold of her arm as she headed down the hallway, and she yanked it away, yelling, "Maybe if you weren't so damned needy, I could stand to look at you twice." As soon as it came out, Sarain knew that she was wrong for saying it; the truth was, she didn't even mean it, but she could see the hurt it put in Winston's eyes, and before she could take it back, she heard him saying, "You know, perhaps if you weren't about as passionate as a rock, Orran would have stuck around instead of running off to be with the horde of demons!"

Sarain struck her hand across Winston's face, slapping him angrily. She then immediately turned away and ran for the door. Winston followed, but was two steps behind her, and as she burst out the door, he stopped short when he saw the blue forming in the sky; daylight was approaching. He glanced out the door and saw that Sarain had already made her way across the field.

He slammed his hand against the frame in frustration, and then let his gaze fall to the ground. His eyes then focused onto spots on the concrete; there on the ground were droplets of water. Winston immediately looked up to the sky, but saw no clouds ahead. He then glanced back to the ground and realized why Sarain had been so quick to leave; it wasn't because she was angry, it was because he had made her cry.

"Damn it!" he shouted, angry with himself. He glanced back out into the approaching day, and wondered how long it would take for Sarain to come back.

Winston woke up in the den a few hours later; he had fallen asleep waiting for Sarain to return. He looked up at his clock hanging on the wall and realized that it was well into the day; Sarain may have already returned while he was sleeping. He got up with a groan and made his way down the hallway. The bedroom door stood slightly ajar, and he quietly pushed it open.

In one quick glance, Winston could see that Sarain had returned home, and had taken with her all her possessions. The room was empty of anything that belonged to Sarain, and it was clear that she hadn't planned on coming back. Winston started searching around the room and then the den for anything she may have left behind, but he found nothing, not even a note.

He let out a strenuous groan knowing that Sarain could be anywhere, even heading out of town. He looked to his heavy cloak and wondered if it would be strong enough this early in the day. He took a deep breath, thinking to himself how he wasn't going to let Sarain walk out on him again.

"Not again," he muttered with a tear falling from his eye.

Chapter 15

Sarain sat at the bus station, her backpack at her side. She held a ticket in her hand, waiting for her bus to come. She had never left a town without finishing her mission before; she felt cowardly as she sat there, but without Orran, she didn't see there being a possibility of defeating her father. Even if he hadn't turned, Sarain knew their chances were slim; she couldn't defeat Aion one on one those years earlier, how could she fight him with his demon army behind him.

Sarain glanced up as the bus rounded the corner on its approach; she began to get up, lifting her backpack onto her shoulder when she felt a moment of hesitation. Aion was the reason she had lost so much, she didn't know if she could spend her whole life running from him, and letting him go unpunished.

The bus stopped in front of Sarain and opened its doors. She looked up into it for a minute with the bus driver staring down at her. Sarain then thought of Winston, he had been sleeping peacefully in his den when she left; she had disrupted his life so much that she wondered if he was better off with her not in it all together. She was tired of breaking his heart, and in fact, it had never been her intention to hurt him so much; even with the demon blood coursing through his veins, he didn't deserve the treatment she gave him.

"Are you getting on?" the tired bus driver gruffly asked. Sarain reached for the bus's sidebar, and took a step on when she felt a wave of energy hit her. She staggered back and looked up at the bus driver with confusion, who appeared annoyed with her hesitation, but none the wiser to why she waited. Sarain glanced around the bus's door, but saw no signs of a barrier. She reached for the sidebar again, and this time had no trouble stepping on board, but before the bus driver could close the door, Sarain heard herself saying, "Wait, I'm not going."

She stepped off the bus, and watched it drive away. As it disappeared into the distance Sarain felt a sickness growing in the pit of her stomach, and she knew that it was something inside her that wouldn't let her leave. Sarain thought of Eddie and the members of her clan; she owed them all, and couldn't let them go un-avenged. Then she thought of Orran fighting on Aion's side, and she swallowed down the urge to vomit; she couldn't bear to face him in battle, but she knew she had no other choice.

If she ran, Aion and his demon army would only track her down. Sarain knew she had to stay, and let things finally play out. She just wondered if she would still be standing in the end.

Sarain walked the small town of Shaven, the sun getting heavy in the sky. She wondered how many of the innocent looking buildings were really just a glamour hiding some kind of dark demonic magic: secret tunnels, portals, magical marketplaces, hidden demon residencies. It seemed like the whole town was just a front for the demonic society that dwelled there. She wondered if even the human population there could be trusted; they too could be keeping their eyes open for Aion. Sarain knew it was a real possibility, if he could get Orran to work for him.

Sarain questioned how long she could keep hidden in the town. She couldn't check into the motel, besides Winston had already found her there once. His place was too predictable, even if it was the smarter choice with its lack of entries and no humans around to be harmed. Though while Winston could provide Sarain with more protection than working alone, a part of her no longer wanted to involve him in her battle; it wasn't fair to keep dragging him into her business, and she didn't want to lose the only semblance of a friend she had left. She felt keeping Winston out of her life and far from her was what was best for him.

Sarain kept her eyes hidden behind a pair of dark sunglasses as she walked the more populated parts of town. Pedestrians passed her without a second glance as she walked aimlessly. As she trekked, she passed a couple holding the hands of a small child between them. The boy caught her eye for a split second, he resembled a younger version of Kit, the boy she had lost so many years ago. As she thought about him, she realized that he would have been in his twenties by now if he had lived to today.

Sarain stopped and closed her eyes for a moment, wondering about the man Kit would have been. He had been in her life so briefly, but Sarain never cared over another person in that maternal way before or since then; it was an experience she would never forget. She had almost abandoned her life's mission for the boy, and often she wished she had. Sometimes she dreamt of a life where she had run those many years ago with Kit, and raised him in some small town. He could have been her brother or something like a son; she could have taught him how to protect himself from the cruelties of the world, and he could have shown her how to live a real life.

It was a hopeless dream that Sarain knew would never happen, but it was a nice dream nonetheless. She raised her hand to her face, and wiped away a tear from her eye.

Sarain glanced over across the street, and saw a bar with its front door ajar and a neon sign glowing, "Open". She wasn't really one to drink, but given the state her life had been in, she couldn't see the harm in letting herself get lost in a drink for a moment. She walked inside to see that the bar was about half full; some couples, some college kid types, and a few loners who seemed to fit the bar's worn down theme.

Most of the booths were taken so Sarain sat down at the bar where she ordered the first mixed drink to catch her eye on the menu. The bartender didn't bother to card her, which Sarain thought was weird since she was aware that her looks hadn't aged in some time, but after examining some of the faces of some of the other patrons in the bar, she realized that under aged drinking wasn't really a concern there.

When her drink came, Sarain stared at it for a moment; it was blue with a maraschino cherry floating at the top. She took a sip and immediately tasted lime followed by a weak hint of alcohol, it was a sweet drink, and not at all what Sarain expected to be drinking in a place like this. She sipped it further until a man came up and sat next to her and said, "That's a chick's drink."

Sarain let the straw slip from her lips as she remarked, "Last I checked I was a woman." The man gave a light chuckle as though Sarain had made a joke rather than an observation, and then he stated, "Seems to me, anyone who comes here to drink alone, man or woman, is going to be drinking hard. It'll take a lot of those to get you hammered." "What should I be drinking then?" Sarain asked curiously. The man turned to the bartender and ordered two drinks. When they arrived he passed one of them to Sarain, saying, "This drink you will feel." She took a sip of it and frowned, "Ugh, that's awful." "That's a man's drink," he said with a chuckle.

Sarain drank the disgusting drink down anyway, and by the third, hardly noticed the after taste. By then she felt more comfortable with the man, who had introduced himself as Sean; he had lived in Shaven for nearly three years and worked in a factory. He looked to be in his mid thirties, and spoke of no family, but Sarain could see a distinct tan line of a missing wedding ring on his ring finger. He was obviously flirtatious with Sarain, though she didn't flirt back, but she continued to accept his drinks. She told him little of herself; however, he seemed more interested in stroking his own ego, bragging about his accomplishments as though they would mean something to her.

After a couple of hours went by Sean suggested they leave the bar together, "Let's take a walk," were his exact words, and Sarain looked at him, feeling no threat from him, and said, "Sure." She followed him out, and they walked down the street. He talked again for a while, still going on about himself, and mentioning something about jealous coworkers. Sarain only half listened to what he was saying; she mostly zoned him out and looked up at the stars. That's when she heard him say, "They really are beautiful." "What?" Sarain asked suddenly acknowledging the man's presence. "The stars are beautiful….but not half as beautiful as you," Sean stated. Sarain nearly rolled her eyes at the comment, thinking how lame it sounded.

Sean then leaned in towards her and tried to kiss her, but Sarain quickly shifted out of his path. "Playing hard to get, huh?" he remarked and then leaned in again. Sarain's eyes then scanned the area and she soon realized that they had walked into a narrow alleyway out of the street's passing view. Sean tried to kiss her again, and

Sarain evaded him once more, but this time he appeared to get aggravated.

"Come on, I bought you all those drinks; they weren't free you know," Sean stated with frustration. "I guess you didn't buy me enough," Sarain muttered, and started to walk away when he grabbed her by the arm. His grip was weaker than what Sarain was used to, but the curiosity in her made her play along; she wasn't used to human violence. She let him push her against the alley wall as he said, "Now I can be nice about this, and we can have some fun, or you can continue to make me mad."

Sarain didn't answer, she just simply stared up at the man with a half smirk on her face. Sean looked at her curiously for a second before saying, "You're just a tease, aren't you?" He then stroked back her hair and leaned in again, and as he went to kiss Sarain she turned her head causing him to kiss her cheek instead. "That's enough teasing," he said as he pressed his weight against her with his hands on her shoulders, trying to pin her to the wall. He started kissing her neck in a half slobbering manner, and then lowered one of his hands to her waist, and tried to work his way under her shirt.

The whole thing felt awkward to Sarain, who was quickly losing interest in the man, and once Sean's hot palm touched her cold waist, she immediately felt disgusted. She wondered how many times this man had done this to other women he had gotten drunk at that bar; women who weren't strong enough to fight off his advances. She wondered if afterwards he planned to go home to the wife whom he was obviously trying to hide by taking off his wedding ring.

He may have been human, but Sean was quickly looking like a monster in Sarain's eyes, and she only knew to do one thing to monsters. Sarain began to feel her eyes burning in her skull, and as she sensed Sean reaching for her breast, she felt herself lowering her mouth to his neck. He moaned for a moment, assuming she was getting into the act by kissing his neck, but the moment didn't last long once Sean realized that Sarain was biting him instead.

He shouted, and Sarain quickly moved her hand out from his grasp, and covered his mouth. She then slammed him against the opposing wall, sending a shock through the man. She let her fangs extend into the man's throat as his blood began to flood into her mouth. He tried to squirm and scream as she swallowed down his blood, and continued to feed on him. Her own skin went hot as Sean's grew clammy. A surge of energy went through Sarain, and the rush caused her to tighten her grip on the man. She noticed that his knees were growing weak, and she held him up when they started to buckle.

She noticed that she could feel his heartbeat slowing, and still she felt nothing but the energy. Sarain closed her eyes, preparing to finish what she had started when suddenly the image of her mother flashed into her mind. She quickly opened her eyes, but the image did not escape her head. She no longer saw the brick wall behind Sean, but instead saw Ariana standing in a field of flowers. She stood as though she had been waiting for her daughter, but as her eyes stared out, she looked up as though she truly was watching Sarain and her actions. Ariana looked appalled as she gazed at her daughter, her hand covering her gasping mouth, and tears escaping her eyes.

She began to turn away from her daughter in disgust, when Sarain quickly broke her lips away from the man's neck, and shouted, "Mom, don't leave!" Sean quickly crumpled to the ground as Sarain eased up on him. Her mother's image began to fade and once again a brick wall stood before her. Sarain pounded her fists against the wall, hoping to bring her mother back, but it was of no luck. She began to cry as she crouched to the ground, not caring that Sean was crawling away. Soon Sarain was in the alley alone, clutching her knees as she cradled back and forth. Tears streamed down her face as she shook and shivered, suddenly feeling very cold.

Sarain felt sick as she realized what she was becoming, and what she had almost done. She felt the sickness rising in her stomach, and she began to vomit; it reeked of booze and blood. She continued to cry as she purged herself of toxins, and when she was done, she sat there quietly weeping.

She heard footsteps slowly approaching, and her first thought was that Sean had come back seeking vengeance, but when she looked up she saw a pair of friendly eyes staring down at her with concern.

"Winston…" she muttered half sobbing. He gazed down at her, glanced at the contents of her vomit, and then back at her; and it was apparent by the look on his face that he knew what had happened. But there was no judgment in his eyes, no, instead he reached down and helped her up, saying, "Come on, I'll take you home."

Sarain stood up and leaned against Winston for balance, suddenly aware of how sick and weak she felt. She clung to him as they walked, and while they made the long trek home, she whispered to him, "I'm glad you found me."

Chapter 16

When they finally reached Winston's place, Sarain was nearly half asleep and ice cold. She felt limp in his arms as he carried her the rest of the way. He helped her to the bedroom and laid her down on the bed, then covered her with several thick blankets to help stop her shivers.

As Winston tucked Sarain in, he heard her weakly ask, "Why do you always help me?" He looked down at the glassy eyed Sarain, and said, "Because with everything you do and have been through, you deserve at least one solid thing in your life that you can depend on." "But I haven't been that loyal to you," she strained herself to say. "That's okay; I haven't earned the right to have the same kind of loyalty and devotion bestowed upon me," he responded. "I don't understand, you've been nothing but unwavering to me," she stated. "Yeah, but only to you; without you I am not the same man. You came into my life and made me want to be a better person, but before you I was a monster, even when I was still a man… That's why I don't deserve the same kind of devotion," he explained.

Sarain sat up and stared at Winston, her eyes still looking hazy, but she spoke very clear as she said, "I am not a saint, and I struggle just the same as you every day with who I am. But you're no more a monster than I, and if we really are beasts than we'll be damned together." Winston stared at Sarain in amazement for a moment, and then watched as she collapsed back on the bed with exhaustion. "You really are the stubborn one aren't you," Winston said with a smirk, "I'll let you get your rest."

He got up from the bed, and began walking towards the door, and as he reached it and began to take his step out, Winston heard Sarain mutter one last thing before she passed out; "I never stopped thinking about you."

He stood still in his tracks for a moment, surprised, but grateful to hear that for once Sarain did feel the same as him; whether her thoughts about him were ones of love or not wasn't clear, but now he realized that during all those years he wondered and longed for her, she was thinking about him as well. Winston let out a sigh of relief, knowing that he did mean something to Sarain.

He closed the bedroom door, and began walking down the hallway when he suddenly felt a draft. As Winston reached the living room he noticed that his door had been left ajar, and he wondered if he had left it that way while focusing on carrying Sarain, though when Winston heard a low growl coming from behind him, he knew that he wasn't the one who left the door open.

Sarain lay there in bed, beginning to drift in and out of consciousness, all the while still feeling a bit of sick in the pit of her stomach. She wasn't sure if it was the booze or blood turning in her, but at that moment she swore off both. She closed her eyes trying to let her body fall asleep, but her mind still raced with completely random thoughts. Suddenly a crashing sound coming from the living room caused Sarain's eyes to shoot open.

"Was that just in my head?" Sarain thought to herself, but then when she heard Winston shout out, she knew that she hadn't imagined it, and she strained herself to get out of bed. She could hear him yelling in pain, and panic began to take over her. She staggered to the door, completely weak and useless, but all she could focus on was getting to Winston.

Sarain leaned against the bedroom door as she turned the knob, and nearly fell as the door swung open with her weight against it. She stumbled down the hallway, trying to rush to the living room; her mind racing with thoughts of what she might find. Once she finally burst into the room, she saw a group of especially large demons gathered there, two of which were holding onto Winston's arms. And standing there in the center of the room was Kayne and his bat-like wings, his back was to Sarain as he faced Winston, and Winston looked as though he had already been smacked around a few times.

Sarain's heart began to race knowing she was weak and unarmed, and that both she and Winston were in serious danger. Winston noticed Sarain standing in the door way first, and tried to signal her to run to the door with his eyes, but she didn't want to leave him behind. A tear escaped his eyes as he signaled Sarain once more to run, but before she could take off one of the demons holding onto him grunted at Kayne, who turned in Sarain's direction.

"Ahh, I see she is here," Kayne stated sounding pleased. Sarain stared over at the large beast with fear and immediately noticed that he was missing an eye; one of his yellow eyes had been slashed away and the scar already looked as though it was healing over; it wasn't fresh. "Grab her!" Kayne suddenly shouted, and Sarain tried to run for the door, but failed when a large demon tackled her to the floor, causing her face to smack against the ground, and for her to bite down into her own lip, drawing blood.

The demons pulled her up, and held her arms tightly behind her back, nearly dislocating her arms out of the sockets. She tried to struggle, but failed to break free in her weakened state. Kayne then approached Sarain, a sword in his hand, and with his free arm, reached up and stroked his clawed hand against her cheek. Sarain flinched at Kayne's icy cold touch; both from chill and disgust. He smiled a creepy toothy smile, as he said, "You really are a beautiful pain in my side."

"Don't you touch her!" Winston quickly yelled, his eyes filled with worry for Sarain. Kayne turned to Winston once again, and said, "You're not in a position to make demands," and then he struck him across the face. Sarain cried out, and Kayne quickly looked towards her with a smirk about his face. He then glanced back at Winston and stated, "So that's what hurts you." Sarain panted, still struggling to break loose, as she stammered to say, "Leave him alone, it's me you want!" "True," Kayne said, "I really have no use for him." And then Sarain watched in terror as Kayne raised his sword and plunged it into Winston's stomach. Time felt as though it had nearly stopped as she stared at the gruesome site, Winston's eyes burned with anguish, and Sarain heard a scream echoing throughout the room, and it took her a moment to realize that the scream was her own.

Dark blood spilled from his mouth as Winston tried to cry out in agony, but he only managed to gurgle up more blood. "Winston!" Sarain screamed with tears falling from her eyes. Kayne ripped the sword away from Winston's gut, and the two demons holding onto him let him go. His body limply fell to the ground, and he didn't move. Sarain screamed again, her eyes burning in her skull, as she tried to break free from the demons' grasp. She got an arm loose and scratched one of the demons across the face, it cried out in pain, and immediately smacked Sarain in the chest, knocking the wind out of her, and grabbing her arm once again.

They began to carry her out of the house, and she struggled to catch a glimpse of Winston. He was lying on the ground in a pool of his own blood, still not moving. Sarain's vision blurred with tears and for a second she could have sworn she saw Eddie lying there. When she looked back, it was Winston's blond hair covered in blood, and his body lying on the ground, and Sarain realized that that sight was much worse for her. Winston was her only friend, and as she stared at him, she felt her heart begin to break.

Sarain's head began to grow light, and her body turned cold. Her vision blurred further until things finally went black with Winston's body being the last thing she saw, and the last thought to go through her head was, "God don't let me lose him."

Chapter 17

Things remained mostly dark for Sarain, except for the occasional blurry glimpse of desert landscape, and then glimpses of a rocky mountain side. Everything had a strange bluish hazy tint to it; the rocks, the dirt, and also the moon, but even in her delirium, she knew that they were taking her to her father's hidden hideout; the one in the cave that she had previously barely escaped from.

Sarain dreaded facing Aion again, and having him look upon her with the same violet eyes that she always tried to hide from the public's view. She couldn't stand seeing the man who had caused her so much pain and grief throughout her life, even before she had met him. She couldn't fathom that the same blood pulsated in their veins; it was like everything she despised about herself and her life came from his tainted demonic blood.

As the demons carried Sarain deep into the dark cavern, her head throbbed with pain, and her eyes had trouble adjusting to the darkness. The tunnels of the cavern began to flash in and out of night vision before her eyes like a faulty flashlight flickering on and off. She glimpsed the back of Kayne's bat wings walking ahead;

his wings were folded in behind him like that of some kind of dark angel rather than that of a bat. His wings looked bony, and contorted, with talons at their ends. He was a formidable beast, and another monstrous spawn of Aion's, and after seeing other outcomes of her father's creations, Sarain wondered if she too was destined to become some monstrosity.

They carried Sarain into a dimly candlelit chamber where a dark figure stood waiting; Sarain lifted her drooping head, and immediately recognized her father. A pleased smile spread across his face when he saw her. She then let her head fall back down, uninterested in anything he had to offer her.

Kayne approached his master, and in his raspy voice said, "We found and retrieved your daughter, Father, and took care of her ally." Aion nodded his head and replied, "I see, you did a good job," then he raised his hand to Kayne's scarred eye, and remarked, "It looks like you have learned your lesson since your last mistake; you know I was displeased to hear of your attack on my girl." Sarain's stomach curdled, something about the way Aion referred to her made her feel uneasy, like he saw her as his possession. She also realized now how Kayne had lost his eye. It wasn't fighting with Winston; it was a punishment from her father for having tried to kill her earlier upon their first meeting.

Aion advanced toward Sarain, who refused to look at him. He took her by the chin firmly with his hand, and forced her head up, so that her eyes would meet his. She immediately spat on his face, and instead of wiping the saliva away, Aion sniffed the air and then smiled. "You have been feeding," he stated, and then turned to Kayne, pleased again, and commented, "Things are going better than I have imagined." He then turned back to his daughter and asked, "Did you kill the poor bastard?" Sarain stared up at him with hatred and refused to answer. Aion studied his daughter's face for a moment and then let her head drop as he released his hold on her, saying, "Of course you didn't," he turned and took a few steps away, and then looked back at her, "But soon you will!" Aion gazed down at her, stating, "Soon you will be as blood thirsty as any beast here, and with that lust to fuel you, and you'll lead my army upon the cattle that plague us."

"You look a lot like one of the cows, yourself," Sarain finally muttered. "Yes, but it's not the shell that makes the beast; it's the power. And my power will be greater once my army can walk in the sun. Without that weakness they no longer have to cower in the shadows, they can finally reign over the weaker species," Aion preached. "Domination over mankind, murder and chaos; is that really what you want?" Sarain sneered with disgust. "They already have murder and chaos all on their own; they are monkeys, they don't deserve to have dominance of this earth. The greater and stronger species should be in control. They live what? Sixty maybe eighty years if they're lucky, well we are much luckier. We can live hundreds, thousands of years; in fact we don't have to have an end date at all," he smiled.

"Your 'creatures' are not superior to humans; they act like brainless rabid animals!" Sarain shouted. "Yes, some do, but none of them obsess over pieces of colored paper, or starve themselves to look how someone else deems beautiful! Sometimes what is primal is better," he responded, "Such pitiful beings don't deserve to have control over the land. If they want to be more than just cattle, they should have to fight for that right just like any other animal does; as we have, and as you have." "What are you talking about?" she asked, confused, and her father replied, "Like you haven't fought against our kind for the right to survive, well that's just precisely what we are doing as well. You've just been fighting for the wrong side, and it's a side that is too weak and too stupid to fight for its self! It may seem noble to fight for those who are helpless, but it has gotten you nothing but trouble and pain. Especially since your god designed the world so that only the strong can survive."

"I don't care how god designed the world; nothing deserves to be killed for killing's sake!" she shouted. "You act as though I'm the devil. You forget that I'm your father; your very existence is because of me." "You killed Eddie!" she cried. "So I took from you someone who wasn't even worthy of you, I've given to you as well," Aion stated matter-of-factly. "What have you ever given me?!" Sarain yelled. "I gave you another chance with your oldest friend," Aion replied, and then glanced past her as someone else entered the chamber.

Sarain glanced up with her eyes as the person walked over to her, and she saw Orran staring down at her. "Sarain," Orran muttered, but she turned away from him; this man was not the friend she used to know.

Aion attentively watched Orran with his daughter, and as Orran knelt next to her and gently lifted her head to him. He whispered softly to her, "Sarain, things aren't how they look; you don't understand all that has happened." But Sarain jerked her head away from him, and then while glaring up at Orran, she said, "They killed Winston!" And then she looked away once again, and refused to say anymore to anyone. Aion scoffed at his daughter's stubbornness, and then looked to the creatures holding her and ordered, "If she wants to be obstinate, then we'll just have to break her of that. Take her to her room!"

'Her room' – the words sounded funny to Sarain, she thought as the beasts dragged her away; Aion was acting like a father punishing a willful teenager. She could feel Orran's eyes on her as she was taken out of the chamber, and could sense his angst that she wasn't glad to see him. Orran had become a stranger to her; worse, he had become the enemy.

Sarain wondered what dank hole of a room they planned to put her in. Likely some dungeon or oubliette, where they would keep her in total darkness until she had gone insane. After a few twists and turns down the many tunnels, the beasts carrying her finally stopped in front of a heavy looking stone door. An iron handlebar lock fixed the door shut, and as one of the creatures lifted the lock and pushed the door open, she heard the door groan and drag. It was a door fitting for a dungeon, and once it was open wide enough, the demons merely threw her in, unconcerned with restraining her; they clearly didn't see her as a threat.

Sarain lifted herself slowly from the ground, her body aching and her knees now feeling bruised, and looked around at her candlelit surroundings. She was amazed to see that besides the stone walls and floors, the room actually looked perfectly normal. There was an oversized bed, a rug, and a wardrobe filled with clothes all in Sarain's size. Candles lit the entire room, making the room almost seem pleasant, but Sarain was not fooled; no matter how Aion tried to dress things up, this was still another room in a den of beasts.

Sarain quickly went to the door and pulled on its iron handle, but it was useless; the door was latched shut from the other side. She then walked over to the bed, and sat down. She looked down at her dirty clothing and then looked over to the wardrobe full of clothes, but shook her head thinking that that was exactly what Aion wanted: for her to make herself at home. She wondered if she should even be using the bed, and then suddenly she was overcome with a feeling of failure. There was no point to anything anymore; Sarain had been captured and there was nothing left to fight for. Anyone or anything Sarain could possibly obtain would only be taken away from her, and she was tired of fighting.

She tried to shake this feeling away, and reminded herself that she had spent most of her life alone already, and that she should not let yet another setback stop her from completing her life's mission: she would put a stop to her father's evil tyranny once and for all. And then she thought of Orran. She wasn't sure what he was, but she was sure that her friend died that day of their clan's massacre those many years ago. And that no matter what that thing using his image tried to say to her, Sarain would sooner die than join her father.

Chapter 18

 A young Sarain danced and twirled in a field of wildflowers, the sun shining down and warming her tanned skin. She chased after butterflies all the while stealing glances from the corner of her eye, watching Orran playing pretend swords using sticks with a couple of other boys.

 Sarain placed a gently made crown of flowers on her head, hoping that Orran would notice her more with it on. She skipped through the flowers pretending to be a beautiful princess, hoping that Orran would want to be her prince. She make believed that Orran was battling his friends for the right to Sarain's hand, but every time she looked over at him, Orran was not paying any attention to her. She wasn't even sure if he knew she was there. Sarain tried skipping higher and twirling faster, hoping to call his gaze to her, but as she spun, Sarain took a misstep and came tumbling down upon her knees. A thorny wildflower scraped against her knee, and Sarain cried out as warm blood came trickling out her wound. As she looked down at her injury, with tears in her eyes, Sarain noticed a shadow come over her, blocking out the sun. She looked up to see a grown Orran standing over her,

extending a hand to her. Sarain looked down at herself
and realized that she was now grown too, though her
knee still bled. She put her hand to it, and felt with her
fingertips that her blood had turned cold, and her skin
was now pale. She gazed back to Orran and realized that
the day had turned to night, and that the sun had now
been replaced by the moon.

She reached up and took Orran's hand, and he
pulled her up to her feet. Then he took her in his arms,
kissing her on her forehead, embracing her tightly, and
whispering softly, "It'll be okay." Sarain held on to him
closely; suddenly finding herself fearful of losing her
dear friend. "What's wrong?" Orran asked, his voice
filled with concern. "He's going to take you away from
me," she muttered, still clinging to him. Orran gazed
down at her; he looked into her eyes and said, "No one
could ever take me away from you." He then leaned
down and kissed Sarain softly upon her lips. His lips
were warm, tender, and moist, and his kiss made Sarain's
whole body quiver. Their lips parted and she was left
staring up at him, silently, and then with a wave of
passion, Sarain took hold of Orran, bringing him down to
her for a lustful kiss. Her lips pressed against his, firm
and roughly, and she pressed herself against him just the
same. Her body pulsated against his, his skin warming
hers. Their clothes seemed to vanish, as well as the moon,
leaving only the two of them floating in a foggy haze.
Soon Orran was on top of Sarain, kissing her neck and
caressing her thighs. Then he was inside of her, rocking
with her, groaning in thriving pleasure. Sarain moaned
and held tightly onto Orran's back, her body shook with

each of his thrusts, and she listened as his breathing turned heavy. His movements became faster, and Sarain's own breathing grew quicker. She could feel Orran's body growing hot as it throbbed against her, and then with a sudden and strange sensation, Orran stopped and collapsed on top of her, his head resting next to hers. There was no climax, and Sarain could feel his skin growing cold. She grew concerned with this sudden turn of events, and muttered into Orran's ear, "Is everything okay?" But he gave her no answer.

Sarain shifted underneath him, becoming more worried by Orran's silence. She then tried to move out from under him when she abruptly felt him pinning her down to the ground. "What are you doing?" she asked him. He slowly raised his head, his movements seeming abnormal, while his face appeared emotionless and shadowy. Sarain saw that Orran's eyes were closed, this unnerved her as a sick feeling of dread came over her. "Orran, what's going on?" But still he didn't answer her; instead he opened his eyes, and stared down at Sarain. His eyes had grown vacant and glassy, but burned with a glow like a soulless beast; they were the eyes of a demon and not her friend's.

Sarain beat her fists against his chest, and tried to knock Orran off of her with no avail. "Get off of me!" she shouted. Orran then lifted his head back while opening his mouth, and exposing his fangs. Sarain screamed while looking up at him and realizing that she couldn't budge him. Fear rang out from her lips as Orran sank his fangs into her neck, breaking her skin. Her thick blood gushed into his mouth, and as he gulped it down Sarain felt herself fading.

A single thought went through her head: where did my Orran go?

Sarain shot up in bed covered in cold sweat. She shivered, reflecting on her dream, and quickly peered around the room. She was alone, but she didn't feel as though she truly was; she sensed eyes on her, she could feel her father near.

Everything in the room looked the same as it did before she fell asleep; in fact, Sarain noticed that even the candles that lit the room looked the same. Despite that they had been burning for hours, the wax appeared to not have burnt down at all. Sarain wondered if this was a power of Aion's or just some kind of enchanted item he picked up at a place like the marketplace in town.

Sarain stretched and rose out of bed, her scrapes and bruises from the events before already appeared to have healed. She wasn't sure exactly how much time had gone by since she was locked in this room, but she sensed that it was night. With nothing else to do, she walked around the room, studying its contents. She glanced inside the wardrobe of clothes, and saw that it was packed with clothes for every occasion, from jeans to gowns, and all in Sarain's size. Some of the gowns looked to be period pieces that laced up instead of having zippers and she wondered if they were authentic and for how long Aion had had them; and even those looked to be her size. Sarain found it a bit creepy that Aion knew her size after not having seen her in years, but then again, he did have Orran reporting to him. Then she noticed something disturbing in the back of the wardrobe. She pushed the other gowns aside, and confirmed her suspicions: it was a wedding gown. Looking at the gown gave Sarain a chill, and she quickly pushed the other gowns back in front of it, also pushing the gown to the back of her thoughts. She then quickly grabbed a set of black sweats, and decided to change out of her filthy clothes. She threw her torn and dirty clothes into a pile in the corner of the room.

Sarain then began to pace around the room, contemplating her next move. She knew she needed to get out of this place, but she didn't know how; she could hear the beasts outside her locked door, guarding the only entrance and exit to her room. There were also likely hundreds of demons in these tunnels, and with them aside, she would still have to worry about facing her father, Kayne, and Orran. She wondered if she would need to first gain their trust to escape, or if she should just make a run for it the first available chance she had…who knew how long she'd be under such close watch.

Sarain's thoughts were interrupted when she heard the latch on her door pop open, and for a moment she had the urge to leap for the door, but stopped once she realized that she wouldn't get far. She would have to play it cool for now, and wait for a better opening to escape.

The door swung open with a groan, and a chill went down Sarain's spine when she saw her father, Aion, step into the room. "What do you want?" she grunted. "To see my daughter, that's all," he replied with a smirk, "I trust you slept well. No bad dreams…I hope," Aion said staring down at her in such a way that she felt as though he knew what she had dreamt.

He then glanced at an oil landscape painting hanging on the wall, while he commented, "I noticed that you're already in the habit of sleeping during the day." "Makes it better for hunting your creatures all night," Sarain remarked. "They're your kind as well, and if I have my wish, they won't be confined to night much longer," Aion responded, "But until then, we need to get you prepared for your new position; I want you to be my second in command." "What, Kayne not doing it for you?" she grunted. "Kayne is strong, but he is a brute; he lacks the skill and grace of a good leader." Sarain rolled her eyes and said, "Like I would ever lead your army." "Perhaps, if they had a strong general leading them, they wouldn't be the animals you hate so much. They could be more controlled, more civilized," Aion preached. "Why would I want them to be anything, but dead?" Sarain replied.

Aion sighed, and thought for a moment before saying, "You could live a real life here; no more running, no more hiding, no more being alone, and no more loss." Sarain looked at him, but said nothing, so Aion continued by saying, "We could be a family." She let out a brief chuckle, but still didn't reply. Aion ignored his daughter's reaction and simply stated, "We need to start your training." "I already know how to fight," she muttered. "Yes, but not well enough, there's still room for improvement," he remarked. Sarain began to grow annoyed, and quickly stated, "If you try to train me against one of your beasts, I'm going to kill them!" "I doubt you'll hurt your trainer," Aion responded, and then he called out, "We're ready for you, come in."

The door groaned open once again, and in stepped Orran. Sarain looked up with a bit of surprise, but more for the thought of how she would once again be training with Orran, like when she was a child. She then looked to Aion and asked, "Seriously?" "Would you rather train with Kayne?" he stated back. Sarain scoffed, but didn't answer. Aion continued with, "Besides, I want you two working together so that you can lead my army side by side." "What, like general and captain?" Sarain remarked. "No, like husband and wife," Aion replied to Sarain's surprise.

Sarain felt her body flush as she tried to get over the shock of her father's words. Her jaw dropped and she suddenly cried out, "You can't be serious?" "I'm completely serious; you two are my greatest creations, of course I want you to rule together... And to breed the next generation of soldiers," Aion answered. "You're crazy!" she shouted. Aion then extended his hand and opened his closed fist to show a pair of wedding rings resting on his palm. "You could have a genuine wedding if you like; keeping with some of the traditions of a normal life," Aion stated. Sarain scoffed at her father once again, and then Orran turned to her and said, "Really, Sarain. We can have a full life together. My love for you is real, and if you give me the opportunity, I'll prove it to you every chance I get."

Sarain stared at Orran in disbelief, but before she could reply, Aion stated, "You don't have to give an answer yet. Take some time to think it over. And in the mean time, you two have some training to do." Aion walked out of the room, leaving Sarain and Orran alone. Sarain gave Orran a quick nervous glance to see that he was staring at her intensively. Sarain felt her body flush again, and couldn't help feeling like a nervous schoolgirl around him, but she couldn't understand why; why did he still make her feel this way even now, while he was her enemy? Sarain couldn't help but still see the old Orran when she looked at him. She closed her eyes and looked away, then muttered, "Let's hurry up and get this training over with."

Chapter 19

Orran led Sarain down one of the many dimly lit tunnels; she remained quiet throughout their walk, and avoided Orran's frequent glances. Sarain wondered about Orran, and how he could follow her father's every order, and then she thought of how as kids, he followed her grandfather, Delmar's, every wish. Orran was always the perfect student, whether it was for good or evil. Sarain just couldn't believe that he joined up with Aion, after what her father did to their people, and she wondered how he could serve him, and why.

They entered a large open area; it was their training room. The walls and floor were made of stone; the whole demon headquarters was built out of the very rock of the mountain it was located in, a feat that must have taken many demons many years to create.

Orran stopped in the middle of the room, and turned to Sarain with a serious look on his face. He then said, "Today I want you to practice fighting with a more calculating technique." Sarain stared at him with puzzlement, and Orran explained, "You have a habit of fighting wild; you jump right into a fight without thinking of what steps you plan to take, and this leaves you open to attacks." "It gets the job done," Sarain quickly stated in her defense. "See, you let your emotions get the better of you. You need to learn to keep your composure," he remarked. Sarain rolled her eyes saying, "Let's just get on with this."

Orran grabbed a sword from a stand, handed Sarain one of her own, and then he got into a fighting stance and raised his sword. Sarain took this moment to suddenly rush Orran with incredible speed, barely giving him time to block her attack. Her blade clanged loudly against his; her sword causing his to chip slightly from the force of impact. Orran hesitated for a moment, in shock from Sarain's aggressive attack, and she took advantage of his mistake, and quickly swung again. He went to block again, but was surprised when Sarain's sword didn't collide with his and instead she stopped in mid swing, and suddenly jumped into the air, bringing her foot up into a high kick. Her foot collided into Orran's face, he stumbled back, but she was surprised to see him still on his feet.

A look of frustration came over Orran's face, and he gruffly stated, "Okay, you've proven your point, now follow direction and get into a starting stance!" But Sarain didn't comply; she quickly rushed Orran again swinging her sword at him, and he quickly moved to block it. Her sword clanged hard against his again, causing it to chip once more. Sarain grunted in frustration as she gripped her sword tightly with both hands forcing it harder against Orran's, and then in a quick second she took one hand off her blade and brought it back in the air and suddenly punched Orran in the face.

"What is your problem?" Orran shouted at her, steaming with frustration at Sarain's antics. "My problem is that you are working with the man responsible for the slaughter of our entire clan!" she hollered, "How can you?" "He's your father!" he yelled back. "That's no excuse, besides he's nothing to you!" Sarain replied.

Sarain swung her sword again, this time it grazed against Orran's stomach, slashing through his shirt and causing him to slightly bleed. It was a superficial wound, but it was enough to make Orran furious. He charged her and swung his blade so hard against hers that it caused his sword to break off at halfway down the blade, but it also caused Sarain's sword to go flying out of her hands. Orran then pointed the jagged edge of his blade at Sarain and sternly asked, "Do you concede?" Sarain stood up straight, and while standing still, she firmly looked him in the eye and replied, "No."

Orran groaned in aggravation, and suddenly threw down his sword. He then glanced up at Sarain, and to her shock, quickly charged at her. He tackled her to the ground, slamming her back hard against the stone floor. The breath knocked out of her and she gasped to catch it again. Orran pinned her to the ground, and suddenly Sarain's dream flashed into her mind. She tried to push him off of her, but failed to make him budge. Sarain glared up at her former friend, and she half expected for him to transform into a beast and attack her like in her dream, but she didn't expect what did happen next. Still angry, Orran met Sarain's gaze; her eyes were lit up and burning into his; he looked down at her furiously, and then grabbed her abruptly by the shirt, and pulled her head and shoulders up until her lips met his. He kissed her rough and firmly, and once it hit Sarain what he had done, she batted Orran away and broke free from his grasp.

Sarain glared at Orran with bewilderment, and after a moment of shock induced silence, she shouted, "What are you?" Orran stared at her with confusion, and answered, "I am your oldest friend, and you're the love of my life." "No," she immediately stated, "You are not my Orran. My Orran died that night along with everyone else!" "Sarain, don't be absurd, of course it's me," he replied with sincerity. She shook her head and shuffled away further from him, "No, if you were really my friend, you wouldn't be trying to force me into a marriage, and wanting me to serve my insane father." "Sarain…" Orran started to say, but Sarain quickly cut him off by shouting out, "Thanks to you, Winston is dead!" Orran looked appalled as he stated, "You know I wasn't there when that happened." "Maybe so, but you're still at fault… You betrayed us," she responded. A tear ran down Sarain's cheek and she quickly looked away. She took another step away from Orran, and muttered, "I want to go back to my room." "You need to eat something," Orran commented. "No, I want to go back to my room now!" she declared. "Fine," he then gave in.

Sarain followed Orran quietly back down the many tunnels, the silence this time was more awkward than the one before. She never lifted her gaze from the floor, and when they finally reached her room, she quickly brushed past Orran and through the door. She closed the door behind her, not wanting him to follow her in. He sighed and latched her door shut, locking her in. Orran looked down at the ground for a moment, and listened to the sound of soft crying coming from the other side of the door. His hand reached again for the latch, but he stopped himself short. He let his hand drop back down to his side, and then whispered softly, "I'm sorry," before he finally stepped away.

Sarain pushed past the crowds of sweaty dancing people as she made her way through the club. The room was large and dark with only a few pulsating lights flickering on and off to light the room. Her eyes couldn't adjust to this lighting, making the faces of the crowd blur to her.

Sarain wasn't sure how she had gotten there, but she was in an old familiar place; a place she had burned to the ground many years ago, the Purge. She was searching desperately for him, and knew that he had to be here somewhere amongst the crowd: Winston.

She caught a glimpse of blond hair within the dark crowd, and she thought, was that him? A flash of bright blue looked back at her; his eyes. "Winston!" she called out, but the figure was moving away. Sarain pressed through the crowd, shoving men and women alike. "Winston!" she cried out again, but he wouldn't stop. Shoulders, elbows, and arms knocked into Sarain as she tried her best to follow him, but Winston seemed to have no problem getting through the crowd. She was losing him.

Suddenly Sarain stumbled and the next thing she knew was that she was picking herself up inside the tunnels beneath the Purge. She glanced around confused for only a moment and then quickly made her way down the long spiraling staircase. He had to be nearby. She raced down the steps that seemed longer than ever before, but she couldn't afford to stop, not even to catch her breath.

Winston where are you, she thought to herself as she finally reached the last step, and there in front of her stood a large pair of stone double doors. Carved into the doors was a crude depiction of a village on fire and its villagers being attacked by what appeared to be demons. Sarain knew that this image held some kind of significance to her life, but to her now, it didn't matter. She instead used her strength to force the heavy doors apart. They groaned and slowly budged against her weight until they opened enough for her to squeeze through.

Sarain panted heavily as she stared over at Winston who stood in an alleyway with rain beating down upon him. The sky was dark blue from the pre-dawn, and she knew that they had to find a safe haven for Winston to take shelter in. She grabbed him by the arm and pulled him along as she said, "We have to hurry to the Velvet Rose before they find us!" But Winston stopped in his tracks, and gazed down at Sarain to say, "No, it's okay. No one is chasing us." Sarain looked up to the even bluer sky and said, "But it's almost dawn, you need to take shelter." Winston took her by the hand and pulled Sarain closer. He wrapped his arms around her and held her to him, and then he whispered, "Everything is going to be alright, we don't have to run anymore."

Sarain let out a sigh of relief, and wrapped her arms around him. She closed her eyes and let herself breathe. She felt the warmth of the sun on her skin and in that moment felt finally at peace. Then she opened her eyes, and saw that she was clinging to a pile of ash that soon collapsed within her arms. Tears fell from her eyes as she cried out in agony, while the ashes blew away with the breeze, down the already dirty alleyway.

Winston...

Chapter 20

Sarain opened her eyes. She lay in bed, damp with sweat, and felt hot as though she was running a fever. Her head ached with a migraine, and she could hear her stomach rumbling; it had been a long while since she had eaten anything.

Sarain sat up, a little woozy, and tried not to think about her dream, but her thoughts couldn't help but wander to Winston..... Winston.

She lifted her eyes from the bed and scanned the room. Soon her eyes settled on a new object inside her space, it was a table full of food. How had she not heard that being brought in? Fruit, bread, meat, sweets, and a pitcher of tea sat on the table. Sarain stared at the food, she was so hungry.

A knock came to Sarain's door, she didn't answer, and the knocker waited a moment before opening the door anyway. It was Orran; he came in slowly, and said, "Sorry to disturb you, but Aion wants us to train again," he then glanced at the table of food, and added, "After you eat and dress, be ready for me to come back and get you." Sarain gazed up at Orran, but didn't respond. Orran waited a second longer, and then left the room. Sarain's gaze then went back to the table of food.

Twenty minutes went by, and once again a knock came to Sarain's door. Orran slowly opened the door again to find Sarain sitting at the edge of her bed dressed. She stood up without a word, and exited the room, then waited in the hall for Orran to take lead. He turned to leave the room and then noticed the untouched table of food. Sarain hadn't eaten a thing. Orran glanced at Sarain with concern, but didn't say a word; instead he led her to the training room, once again.

Sarain didn't speak to Orran throughout the trip, in fact the first words out of her mouth weren't spoken until they reached the training room, and Sarain saw Kayne standing against the wall. "What is he doing here?" she asked with annoyance. Kayne's yellow eye focused on Sarain as he hoarsely spoke, "I'm here to make sure you stay in line." Sarain rolled her eyes. Kayne's attention turned to Orran and he asked, "Where were you earlier?" Orran avoided Kayne's stare as he muttered, "Just because you're stuck here during the day, doesn't mean that I am. Or have you forgotten that I can go about freely during the day?" A look of contempt came over Kayne's face as he glanced at Orran, but he made no reply.

Orran then took a hold of a katana blade and tried to hand it to Sarain, who simply glanced at it, but didn't take hold of the sword. Orran looked down into Sarain's eyes and whispered, "You need to go along with the training." His eyes pleaded with her, as though he knew something that she didn't, but still she refused to take the sword. Sarain turned to walk away when Kayne stepped in front of her, "Either you train with him or you train with me, either way, you're not leaving here without a few scrapes from a battle," bellowed Kayne as he stared down at Sarain with a sinister look in his one good eye. Sarain gazed up at Kayne and muttered, "Why don't you get Orran to play with you, I'm too tired today." She began to move past Kayne when he suddenly shifted back into her path, he then gazed down at her for a long moment, his view lingering on her breasts, then her neck, and finally her eyes. "If I'm going to 'play' with anyone, be assured, it's going to be you," Kayne replied perversely.

Sarain quickly brought her hand back, and slapped Kayne across the face. The hit didn't even cause him to budge, as his skin was much like a shell, but after a moment, Kayne brought his clawed hand up to his cheek to find that he was bleeding. Sarain's slap had left behind four deep scratch marks on Kayne's face. A look of anger came over him, and Kayne quickly grabbed Sarain's hand to discover that her nails were about two inches long and had turned black. "When did this happen?" Kayne asked, addressing his question more to Orran than Sarain. "I don't know," Orran said with surprise. "Well, make sure you let the Master know!" Kayne ordered, and then he turned his attention back to Sarain. He threw down her hand and suddenly grabbed her by the throat, this caused both Sarain and Orran to flinch; Sarain out of surprise and Orran out of concern. "I don't care if you are the Master's daughter, you try something like that again and I'll…." But Kayne was suddenly cut off; he had begun to pull Sarain up closer to him as he spoke when suddenly something fell loose from underneath Sarain's shirt. His eye focused on the shiny object, and he hissed as he realized that an ankh burned at his hand right in front of him.

Kayne loosened his hold on Sarain's neck and she fell to the ground. Kayne let out a roar of anguish, and immediately yelled, "Has she been wearing that this whole time?" He turned to Orran and ordered, "You can touch them; so get rid of it!" Orran rushed to Sarain's side, he gave her a quick once over to make sure that she was alright, and then reached around to the back of her neck to unclasp the chain for her ankh. He mouthed to her the words, "I'm sorry," knowing that the pendant had once belonged to her mother. Orran took the ankh away and stood back up. Kayne then walked over, grabbed Sarain, and quickly jerked her back up. He glanced at Orran as he stated, "You destroy that while I take her back to her room!"

Orran shot Kayne a look of distrust, he didn't like the idea of Kayne being left alone with Sarain, but he didn't dispute the order either. Kayne dragged Sarain away with her shooting Orran a quick look of betrayal before he left her sight. Kayne pulled Sarain by her arm as he led her back to her room; the trip seeming much faster than when Orran had retrieved her. Once they reached her door, Kayne threw her in and she expected for him the slam the door behind her, but he didn't. Instead he stepped in and closed the door behind himself.

Sarain stared up at Kayne with unease in her stomach. "You know my father doesn't want you touching me," she quickly stated, "He already took your eye, because of your behavior." "So suddenly, you're daddy's little girl?" Kayne responded with a creepy grin, "You're not so tough without a man in your corner." "I'm still strong enough to take you on," she replied. "Not from where I stand... No, you just look like a scared little girl," he stated. Sarain glared at Kayne and stood her ground, he then gave her another eerie toothy smile. And suddenly Kayne came rushing towards Sarain, he slammed her against the wall, and pinned her to its stone. His foul breath beat against her skin, and he whispered into her ear, "Do you know how long it's been since I've had a woman... I mean a real woman, one that doesn't break under this hard body of mine? I think, being the master's daughter and all, you might have it in you to take what I can give," Kayne then licked Sarain from the base of her neck and up to her face, and then he added, "But then again, who knows, you might be like all the others." He gave her one last smile before taking a step back. Kayne then walked out of Sarain's room, locking the door behind him. She could hear him laughing as he left down the hallway, away from her door.

Sarain wiped away, in disgust, the saliva that lingered on her cheek as her eyes burned at the door. Oh how she hated Kayne, and swore to herself that one day she would even the score.

Little Sarain sat playing by the creek; she danced her doll in and out of the water, making the doll splash back and forth. She had a mischievous smile on her face, she wasn't supposed to be playing so close to the water, it was a rule that both her mother and grandfather insisted on, but as of that moment neither was around to see her play.

The gentle breeze that blew suddenly kicked up, and a rippling wave came at Sarain and splashed against the girl's body. It wasn't strong enough to pull her in, but it was enough to get her attention. She quickly glanced down to the bottom of her dress, and saw that it was wet and muddy. In a panic, worrying that her transgression would be found out, Sarain franticly began rubbing at the mud, trying to wipe her clothes clean, but it was of no use; the dirt only further smeared. Sarain let out a defeated whimper and then got up to leave the creek and let her mother know what she had done, when she realized that something was missing; her doll. Sarain quickly looked down the river to see that her favorite doll was hastily floating away. She let out a shriek and started moving further into the water herself, when suddenly she felt a pair of hands on her shoulders.

The girl glanced back to see her mother's concerned face staring down at her. "Mommy, my doll is getting away," Sarain cried. Ariana gave her daughter a sad frown as she told her, "Let it go, baby. It's too far down the river." Sarain turned her attention back to her doll, floating down the river, and shouted, "No mommy, she's my favorite!"

Sarain suddenly dashed into the river for the doll, breaking free from her mother's firm grasp. In fact, Ariana stumbled back, surprised by the strength of her young daughter. After a moment, she managed to catch her breath and mustered the strength to grab her daughter again, this time lifting her out of the water. Sarain cried as she saw her doll disappear down the river, now too far from her view. Ariana sat her down on the soft grass, away from the riverbank. She wiped her daughter's tears and then gave her a gentle kiss on top of her forehead. Sarain let out a whimper, and Ariana softly shushed her and said, "It's okay, sweet girl. I know she was your favorite, but it wasn't safe to go after her." Sarain looked up at her with teary eyes and asked, "Will you get me another, mommy?" Ariana thought for a second before replying, "Actually, I think I have something better to give you."

Ariana at that moment reached around to the back of her neck and unclasped her necklace, and then she leaned toward her daughter, and clasped the chain around Sarain's neck. Sarain looked down at the pendant, and exclaimed, "Mommy, your ankh! Grandma gave you this, it's your favorite!" "I know; that's why I want you to have it," Ariana spoke and then added, "It'll keep you safe, and it'll remind you that sometimes we lose things when we're not ready to have them gone, and sometimes there is something even better waiting for us when we let go."

Sarain smiled sweetly up at her mother, happy to have the pendant, but not fully understanding her mother's words. Ariana stared down at her innocent daughter, gazing into the girl's violet eyes, and for a moment she felt fear: Fear, not of her daughter, but for the uncertain future that lay waiting for the child. Thinking of the incredible strength she had witnessed from her daughter just minutes earlier, Ariana wondered what, other than Sarain's unique eyes, had the girl received from her father. Only time would tell.

     Sarain opened her eyes, she was cold and it felt like morning. She thought about closing her eyes again and sleeping until early evening, which was when the day really began for those who lived in this underground dwelling, but then she decided against it. She couldn't get past how cold she was to be comfortable enough to sleep again, and then she realized why. A cold draft blew through the room through a gap left in her now opened bedroom door. Sarain peered at the door ajar, surprised not only by the carelessness of her opened and unguarded door, but also by the fact that she had not heard anyone open the door or enter her room while she slept.

     She wondered if it was a trick, a mistake, or even a sign that her father was beginning to trust her. Sarain slowly got out of bed, half expecting for something to jump through the doorway, and half to not make noise that would draw attention to the unlocked door. Sarain wondered if Orran could have come by and unlocked her door, and if so, why hadn't he stayed or woken her? Could this be some sort of sick game of Kayne's?

Sarain peered out the door and saw no one standing guard. She also heard no sounds of anyone nearby, and these stone-lined hallways echoed throughout. She stepped lightly out of her room and crept down the hall, stopping to listen for sounds of anyone or anything that could be approaching her location. Sarain debated on what to do; should she go back to her room, should she walk about as if normal and try to find someone, or should she make a run for it? Running would be dangerous; these tunnels were like a maze, and Sarain could easily get lost or caught, and even if she could make it out, where would she go? There was no safe place in town, and she had no one to help get her out of town fast and quietly. Then Sarain thought of her options if she stayed; she could join up with the demon brotherhood, marry Orran, and follow out with her father's plans to lead his demon brothers and dominate over mankind, or she could fight off Aion's plans to control her until he either broke her or she withered away and died.

It took Sarain only a moment to decide, she knew that she could never stomach working side by side with her father; not after what he did to her clan, to Eddie, and to Winston. She would rather risk death, than spend an eternity becoming and leading those which she has spent her life fighting. Sarain would run, or die trying.

Chapter 21

Sarain steadily crept her way through the tunnels, praying that her senses were leading her in the right direction. She had been so disoriented when she was brought to this demonic headquarters, but she could still remember shifts and turns that were made as she was carried in; or at least she hoped that she was remembering correctly. Surprisingly most of the tunnels were lit by torches that burned without putting off any heat; in fact Sarain was almost certain that if she were to touch the flames that she wouldn't get burned; these torches appeared to be another enchantment. She wondered why the demons even bothered with lighting the tunnels, the creatures should have all had well developed night vision; perhaps it was more for show.

Sarain was also surprised that she still hadn't ran into any demons, and she wondered if perhaps they had assembled for a meeting. Given it was day, the usual time that beasts slept, she was sure some of them would be required to be awake for guarding purposes. Nevertheless, she continued on her path until she turned into a tunnel that was not lit by torches. The tunnel seemed to stretch endlessly into darkness, and though

Sarain had no real reason to believe so, she felt as if this was the way out. She walked into the dark abyss, her eyes quickly adjusting to the lack of light, and hurried her steps sensing that her journey was growing ever closer to an end. The tunnel wound like all the others, but this one was dark and damp more like that of the cave it was and not the enchanted headquarters it hid. The ground turned to dirt and pebble rather than stone, and the walls dripped with sludge. This tunnel was definitely less decadent, but it held a sort of peaceful charm for Sarain as she realized that she had seen this tunnel before; it was the same one she had previously went through with Winston and Orran, when they had snuck into the headquarters. Now she was certain she was going the right way, and was fairly sure that she could still remember the way out.

Sarain once again rounded another corner, and this time she could literally see the light at the end of the tunnel; the entrance to the cavern lay only yards away, with daylight beaming in at its opening. Sarain took a deep breath and mustered her strength, and then she began to run. Racing to the exit, she felt her fears begin to fade and hope returning. She ran as quickly as her weak and tired feet would allow, and as she was nearly able to feel the sun on her skin, a sudden yank on her ankle caused her to immediately go crashing to the ground. Sarain was unaware of what had caused her to trip, but as she turned back to discover, she was immediately met with the gaze of a single glowing yellow eye. Kayne snarled at her, he had apparently chased after her on all fours, with the tunnels walls being too narrow for him to fly. But she hadn't heard him following her; he must have been waiting somewhere hidden at the cavern's entrance, waiting for Sarain to attempt to escape.

It was a trap, Sarain thought to herself, and she had just failed.

Sarain went crashing down onto the stone floor of a small dungeon like room, her face hit hard against the ground, splitting her bottom lip open. Kayne had dragged her to this new room, throwing her in upon arrival. Sarain began to get up, trying to make a run for the door when Kayne quickly knocked her back to the ground, and kicked her repeatedly in the stomach. He closed the door as she groaned, struggling to raise herself up. Sarain coughed up blood as she glared up at him and said, "My father is going to be furious when he finds out what you're doing…. He'll take your other eye!" Kayne laughed, a rather demonic sounding laugh, and then replied, "Do you really believe that every man is at your disposal? You human women, so full of vanity!" "It has nothing to do with vanity. I am your master's daughter, and you are just his lackey! Who do you really think ranks higher to him?" Sarain stated, and then spat her bloody saliva at Kayne, hitting him directly in his one good eye. Kayne immediately brought his clawed hand back and smacked Sarain across her face, before wiping his own face off.

Kayne then grabbed a set of chains that lay on the ground attached to a wall. He grabbed Sarain by the wrist and she struggled with him as he tried to fasten them on her. She kicked, scratched at his face, hollered, and bit at Kayne as he chained her hands and feet; in the end, she was no match for him in her weakened state. And as Kayne latched the last chain's cuff around Sarain's ankle, she suddenly heard the room's heavy door groan open. She looked up groggily to see Aion standing in the doorway, a stern expression on his face. Sarain let out a weak laugh as she said, "You're screwed now!"

Kayne turned around to see his master at the door, then gave him a wicked grin as he announced, "I stopped her from escaping just like you asked… You were right about her trying to run if we gave her more freedom." Sarain felt her heart drop as she realized that her last hope had fallen through; Aion wasn't going to save her, in fact he had orchestrated the whole thing.

Aion stared down at his daughter, shaking his head, and said, "I'm very disappointed in you, Sarain. I don't understand why you just can't comprehend that this is your home now. Why do you insist on always running away from me?" Sarain stared up, shakily, at her father, and spoke, "You ruined my life; you've taken everything I've ever cared about from me. Why on earth would I ever want to stay with you?" "Because I'm willing to give you so much more: power, strength, an army, a family," stated Aion. "I don't want to be a part of your twisted family, it's bad enough that your putrid blood pulses in my veins!" Sarain shouted at him. Aion slapped his daughter against her already bruised cheek, and said, "You need to learn to respect me, even if you can't love me! I am your father, your master, your ruler, and your god! And you're not leaving this room until you understand that!" Sarain let out a sad chuckle as she muttered to him, "I guess I won't be leaving this room." Aion glared down at his daughter and replied, "Perhaps not," he then looked to Kayne, and stated, "Do what you need to make her more compliant." Aion then stepped out the room closing the door behind him. Kayne's gaze went to Sarain, and a sinister grin spread across his face.

Hours went by with Kayne hitting, kicking, scratching, and biting at Sarain. Sometimes he would make demands for Sarain to acknowledge her father as her master, and sometimes Kayne just tortured Sarain for the fun of it. Though even with all the pain and beatings, Sarain never complied with Kayne's demands; in fact she barely made a sound, and when she did it was only to curse Kayne for his existence and to belittle him.

Again the heavy door swung open with a groan, and again it was Aion who stood in the doorway. He gazed down at his battered and bloody daughter, and asked Kayne, "Have you made any headway yet?" "No," Kayne grumbled, saying, "Your daughter is stubborn… She should have broken by now." "She's strong like her old man," Aion stated with a smirk. "Give me a few more hours, and I'll have her begging to be by your side," Kayne declared. "Not just yet, I have another idea," Aion responded, he then went to the door and called someone inside. Within moments the door opened again and in walked Orran. His eyes bulged as soon as he saw the bloody Sarain, and he quickly turned to Aion and remarked, "You said that you wouldn't hurt her!" Aion shrugged, and then replied, "And 'I' didn't."

An angered look came over Orran's face, but he didn't say anything else to Aion; instead, he knelt down by Sarain's side and asked, "Are you okay?" Sarain stared up at his concerned face with an intense glare as she replied with blood seeping from her swollen lips, "I'm just peachy." "Just do as your father asks, and this can all be over with," Orran pleaded with her. Sarain turned her gaze from Orran to Aion as she stated calmly, "I'd rather die first."

Aion stared back at his daughter for a moment, a serious look on his face as he seemed lost in thought, and then he turned to Kayne and said, "Well you heard the woman." Orran's heart began to race and he quickly stood up and shouted, "No wait, you need to give her more time!" He looked Aion boldly in the eyes as he requested, "She's tired and weak, making her only want to give up instead of giving in. She needs time to think things over… And she needs food."

Aion took a second to think, and then remarked, "True, I don't think she has eaten since being here; she didn't touch the food brought to her the other day," Aion exchanged glances with Kayne and ordered the beast, "Retrieve her something to eat!" Kayne nodded to his master, and immediately left the room.

Orran knelt by Sarain's side once again and whispered to her, "See, everything is going to be alright, you don't have to fight them. We can all live together peacefully." Sarain stared up at Orran, looking frail and weak, and then she muttered, "You are such a fool!" Orran stared at Sarain shocked by her harsh words, but before he could respond to her, his attention was distracted by the sounds of whimpers and struggling coming from outside the door. Both he and Sarain looked to the doorway as the door opened and Kayne stepped in carrying a woman. The woman was young, pale, and blond, and she would have been pretty if her face wasn't filled with fear. Kayne threw the woman down just as Orran began to stand up and ask, "What's going on?" Aion glanced at him as he replied, "You said it yourself; Sarain needs to eat." "No this is not what I meant, and you know it!" Orran shouted.

Sarain's gaze went to the young woman as she herself realized what her father was getting at. She looked up at the woman's tearful green eyes, and in that second, she recognized them, "Julianne," Sarain muttered groggily. Orran's face became even more appalled as he yelled, "She knows her!?" Aion turned to Kayne and gave him a quick nod, and immediately, Kayne grabbed a hold of Orran and shoved him out of the room. Kayne quickly locked the door, locking Orran out as he pounded on the door from the other side, shouting, "No!" and begging for them to stop.

Aion then unlatched his daughter from her chains. He took her face into his hands, and while staring into Sarain's eyes, he told her, "It's time for you to feed." "No," Sarain replied. "This is not a choice," Aion remarked, "Now eat your friend's little whore!" Sarain rolled her eyes asking, "Is there anything you don't know about?" "Do you think Kayne didn't do his research when he learned where you were staying?" Aion questioned, and then added, "This should make it easy for you; you know she likes to be bitten, she's been feeding that pathetic vil sang!" "I won't do it!" Sarain shouted. Aion glared at his daughter and ordered, "Kill the tramp!" "No!" Sarain protested.

Julianne shook with fear, sobbing loudly, her eyes pleading with Sarain for help, but she was too afraid to speak. Aion glared at his daughter, and then his gaze shifted to Julianne. Sarain saw this and she immediately struggled to get up, shouting, "No!" in the process, but she was too late. Aion swiftly grabbed a hold of Julianne and instantly broke her neck without so much as a struggle from the girl. Sarain dropped to her knees, and sobbed at her failure to save Julianne. Aion stared down at her for a moment, unaffected by his daughter's pain, and then said, "You still have to feed." Sarain gazed up at Aion in disbelief, saying, "You can't be serious?" And before she knew it, Aion had moved with incredible speed; slicing Julianne's neck open with his long sharp nails, and shoving her bloody throat into his daughter's stunned mouth. He quickly grabbed a hold of the back of Sarain's head, not letting her move away as she gagged and choked on Julianne's thick blood. It poured down her throat like syrup, and when Aion finally decided that his daughter had had enough, he let her go.

Aion expected for Sarain to be livid with him, but he didn't expect to see what happened next. Sarain's eyes began to glow, but this was to be expected after feeding; what wasn't, was the fact that Sarain's body began to thrash. Her eyes burned in her head, and her skull felt on fire. Sarain could feel herself losing control of her body, and everything began to blur. Her head whipped back and forth uncontrollably, and tremors moved throughout her body. Her hand shot out and hit Aion, causing him to surprisingly stumble back, dropping Julianne's corpse in the process. Kayne watched in disbelief, also shocked by this unforeseen result, and especially surprised to see that Sarain was able to knock back her father, and though he didn't know why this had happened, he already knew what this meant.

Aion stared down at his daughter, and waited as her seizing slowly tapered off; he then knelt by her side, and gazed down at the motionless Sarain who stared up blankly at nothing. "Sarain?" he said while taking her hand, "Are you still in there?" Aion stared down into her vacant eyes for a moment, before finally letting her hand drop from his. He stood up with a sigh, and turned to Kayne, and said, "It looks like she's just another failure after all."

Chapter 22

Orran sat on the cold stone floor, leaning against the wall, waiting for something, anything to happen. His eyes stayed fixed on the dungeon door as his fears consumed him. The room was quiet, so much so that Orran dreaded that Aion had finally lost his patience with his daughter and done away with her.

Orran's hands ached from pounding against the door, hoping to make it budge, but it didn't. He thought about his friend inside, being forced to feed on an acquaintance. It was an act that Aion had once forced upon him as well, several years ago, only to discover that Orran didn't need to feed on blood, much like Aion himself. But it was a memory that nonetheless, Orran could never forget.

Aion had brought a young woman to Orran's chambers one night; a girl, barely eighteen, ripe with beauty, and with an ample body to match. The girl had appeared to be enchanted or perhaps under some kind of thrall. Once they were alone, she seduced Orran, and when he was amidst in bedding her, Aion suddenly appeared as if out of thin air. He immediately slit the girl's throat, and held Orran down as her blood poured into his mouth. This was both the first time Orran had seen how twisted Aion could be, and when he realized how strong Aion was without really having to try. But even with all that, Orran had still believed that Aion would never hurt his own daughter; her very existence was miraculous, and she was the only real child Aion had ever had. Aion had spent decades tracking Sarain down, and preaching how perfect a creation she was. So when Orran saw the torture Aion had bestowed upon his daughter that very day, his shock was genuine.

Orran's head lifted quickly when he heard the dungeon's door unlock and then the door groaned open. Aion stepped out, a look of disappointment was on his face. He glanced at Orran, and then walked by him without so much as a word. Kayne stepped out next, and Orran could see Sarain's blood was still on his fists. Orran glared up at Kayne, but Kayne ignored this attempt of aggression by stating in a simple nonchalant tone, "You can have what's left of her," he then shook his head and added, "What a waste, and I was hoping to have some fun with that one." Orran looked at him with disgust, he so wanted to beat the smugness out of Kayne, but his concerns now weighed heavy for Sarain. Orran brushed past Kayne as he hurried into the room. His eyes first saw the body of the girl, Julianne; she lay lifeless on the ground. Orran immediately noticed that her throat was void of fresh bite marks, but her neck had been slashed, and he knew this meant that Sarain had refused to feed on the girl of her own freewill.

Then Orran's eyes settled on Sarain, she lay motionless on the ground, staring up vacantly, at the ceiling. Orran quickly rushed to her and knelt down by her side. "Sarain!" he said as he gently shook her, as if trying to wake her from a sleep, but Sarain didn't respond. He put his ear to her chest, and listened for a heartbeat. It was faint, but a weak heartbeat was there. Orran glanced her over; he then wiped away the blood on her mouth with his sleeve, hoping that making her feel more comfortable would help her in some way. Finally he scooped her up into his arms, and then proceeded to carry Sarain back to her room.

Orran passed a few beasts while carrying Sarain through the tunnels; it was night time, and demonic life was busy there underground at this hour. Their red eyes glanced at Sarain as Orran moved by, and he caught a few glimpses of grins on the demons' faces; many of these creatures had hated the idea of a hunter one day ruling over them, and none of them felt the slightest upset over the development of Sarain's wellbeing. Orran ignored the creatures, knowing that any disobedience on his part at this time would not be tolerated. He continued taking Sarain back to her room, and when he reached her door, he kicked it open and angled Sarain inside.

Orran placed her on the bed, and pulled a blanket out to cover her. Sarain's violet eyes still stared blankly out into space; Orran slowly brought his hand up to her face, and gently closed her eyes for her. He muttered, "You need your rest," and then he moved from the bed to a chair where he sat and waited. Orran was afraid to leave Sarain alone; he didn't know what else her father may have in store for her, and he didn't trust the beasts that dwelled there to leave the helpless Sarain alone.

Orran stared at his defenseless friend, and knew that he too was at fault for her condition; he never should have blindly followed Aion, but he felt indebted to him for both bringing Sarain back into his life, and for giving him his life back so many years ago.

The flames of the fire licked at her skin, and seared it off; her hair, her clothes; all gone. Engulfed in flames, with her own body ablaze, she struggled to hold on to him. She could not let him go. Her scorching embrace brought warmth to his heart. He never wanted this for her, but in the end, he was glad he was not alone.

Orran suddenly opened his eyes, realizing that he had fallen asleep. Hours had gone by, and it was day time once more. He looked up to Sarain who still laid there in bed, and he noticed that her eyes were open again, and staring off into space. He then got up and walked closer to Sarain, wanting to examine the state of his friend. Her eyes looked glassy and vacant as Orran sat there on the edge of the bed, gazing down at her. He watched her with worry in his heart, seeing the girl he knew fading away. She looked pale and thin. Hoping that Sarain may have become more coherent, Orran leaned down toward her and muttered softly, "Are you hungry? Would you like me to get something for you?" He stared down at her, but she didn't answer.

Orran sighed then brought his hand down to Sarain, and brushed her hair back, away from her face. He flinched and quickly brought back his hand when he noticed what her hair had been hiding; her ears had become pointed, and they were not at all subtle. His heart began to race as Orran realized that he was quickly losing his friend to something more sinister than he had initially imagined. He then began to shake Sarain and say, "Come on, you need to snap out of this! Being this way isn't good for you!"

Surprisingly, Sarain moaned, but didn't speak. Her eyes shifted towards Orran, but didn't focus on him, and he wasn't even sure if she knew he was there. "That's it, you need to sit up, and eat something," Orran stressed. He reached for her hand, and fished it out from underneath the sheets. He pulled her up, pulling her hands toward him. His eyes went to Sarain's nails; they had turned black, which he had seen before, but now they appeared thicker, as though they were turning into claws.

Orran's heart continued to race as he stared at Sarain and shouted, "Damn it, Sarain, wake up!" He shook her furiously and cried, "Sarain, you have to come back to me, I love you too much to see this happen to you!" He saw her eyes flicker, and then suddenly focus on him. Orran felt her cold skin beginning to warm up, and he gazed down into Sarain's eyes hoping to coax her back into reality. She stared up at Orran and her eyes began to glow.

"Sarain," he said softly, unsure of what was going through her mind. He leaned down toward her, but stopped short when he heard a low growl coming from her. Orran then moved back from her when he saw her expose her fangs. "Sarain!" he shouted at her, "Stop it! This isn't you!"

Suddenly, she shot up in bed and grabbed at Orran; with her left hand she missed, but with her right hand she sunk her nails into his shoulder. Orran groaned in pain and shoved Sarain away from him. She tried to grab at him again, and he quickly slapped her across the face. A tear escaped Orran's eye, and he grabbed Sarain firmly by her shoulders so that she couldn't move. He began to cry as he looked at her and said, "I'm so sorry, Sarain, I never wanted to hurt you. I just wanted to be with you. I've always loved you, and ever since that night our people died, I've been searching for you. I did horrible things in order to find you; to have your father trust me enough to let me be a part of your life again... You were my best friend, Sarain... And I couldn't protect you."

Orran cried as he held onto Sarain, he lowered his head in shame and loosened his grip on her. Her eyes still glowed, but her face softened. Her fangs retracted, and her mind began to clear.

Sarain then saw her helpless old friend in tears, and instinctively broke free of his grasp and wrapped her arms around him. He trembled in her arms and she softly shushed him to soothe his pain. Sarain stroked his hair and whispered, "It's okay, you found me... I'm here now."

She rocked with Orran; back and forth, comforting him, and knowing that he too had lost his childhood and innocence that same night she had lost hers.

Sarain may have been born into this life, but Orran had had it forced upon him just as much as she. She could never punish him for wanting to survive, and for trying to cling to the only family he had left: her.

Chapter 23

Orran held on to Sarain for a long moment, and when he finally pulled away, he looked her in the eyes and said, "I need to get you out of here… We have to escape." Sarain gazed tiredly back at him and replied, "I've already tried that once, remember." Orran shook his head and responded, "But they were expecting it then, now they think you're comatose." "But I'm too weak, can't we wait?" Sarain remarked. "No it has to be now, if Aion realizes that you're coherent again, he's not going to stop trying to test you and turn you to his side," Orran proclaimed. Sarain sighed, and then replied, "Okay… When should we leave?" "Now," Orran said, "It's day time, so most of them should be asleep, and no one should be expecting for you to try to escape again… I'll grab us some weapons, as backup." "Are you sure about this?" Sarain quickly asked. "Yes," he responded, "You wait here… Lie still, and pretend to be comatose until I get back just in case."

Orran turned to leave, but then stopped, he turned back around towards Sarain, walked over to her and gave her a quick kiss on the cheek. "For luck," he whispered to her. He had wanted more from Sarain; he had wanted to feel her lips on his, but Orran knew that that was a privilege that he would have to earn again.

He left the room, and Sarain waited there, quietly, in bed. As she waited, she thought about everything that had happened, and was glad to once again have her old friend back. She now understood why Orran was the way he was, he had spent the greater portion of his life stuck serving Aion, which was a hell that Sarain was trying her best to avoid herself. It was nice for Sarain, knowing now, that she was no longer alone, but she couldn't help but have her thoughts wander back to Winston. The man had given up everything, more than once, to protect Sarain. Her presence always seemed to completely disrupt his life, but he never gave it a second thought; he had blindly loved her. Sarain was worried that Orran was going to suffer the same fate as did the other men who entered in her life, and she knew that she could not bear to lose another.

Sarain suddenly heard her door groan open, and she stayed very still with her eyes closed, not sure who it was that had entered her room. Then she felt the visitor take her by the hand, and say, "It's time to go." It was Orran. Sarain opened her eyes, and he handed her a blade, and then he pulled her up. Sarain was still a bit unsteady on her feet, but she did her best to creep quietly out the room. Orran led the way, as they made the same long trip to the entrance of the cave that Sarain had made the day before.

Sarain's legs ached with every step, and she worried that she was causing them to move too slowly, but Orran did not want to rush her. They traveled far through winding tunnels, and Orran had to help Sarain down several stairs. Eventually, Sarain staggered with her arm around Orran's shoulders; her legs wanting to give out.

Finally, they reached the last long dark tunnel, and nearing its end, Sarain could once again see the light at the end of it. And as they shuffled through, she wondered where it was that Kayne had been hiding the day before. Suddenly, Sarain felt Orran stumble, it was only a minor trip over a rock that he had missed being thrown off by the extra weight of Sarain on his shoulders, but it was enough to cause Sarain, in her weakened state, to toss back her head. Her head bounced back causing her eyes to shoot up towards the cavern's ceiling, and among the stony spikes of the cave is where Sarain saw it; the bright yellow glowing eye of Kayne, watching and waiting while hanging upside down from above.

"Kayne!" Sarain shouted to warn Orran, but it was too late; the beast was already swooping down on them, knocking them both to the ground. "I knew it! I knew you couldn't be trusted," Sarain heard Kayne roar out to Orran. She then glimpsed Kayne picking Orran up and tossing him against the stone wall of the cave. She scrambled for the sword that had fallen from her hand, hoping to be able to come to Orran's aid. When her fingers nearly reached the blade's hilt, Sarain suddenly felt something jerk back hard on her head, and realized that Kayne had taken a hold of her by her hair. Her eyes stared up at the monster helplessly, and as Kayne glared down at her, she heard him say, "That beauty of yours sure has a habit of getting men to bend to your will!" He then raised his clawed hand up to Sarain's cheek, and dug his talons deeply into to her skin as he scratched down her face. Sarain screamed in pain, but was soon drowned out by Kayne's own howl. She felt him let go of her hair, and she quickly moved away to see Orran on his feet, and cutting off one of Kayne's wings.

A bloody stump was left in place of the wing, and as Kayne painfully tried to swat Orran away, Orran abruptly sank his blade into his other wing, nailing Kayne to the ground, with the sword deeply imbedded into the rock. Orran then rushed to Sarain's side, scooping her up as she clung to her sword, and shouted, "No, we have to kill him first!" "No time," Orran quickly said, "The other demons are coming!"

Orran raced down the tunnel, carrying Sarain out, and not stopping even when they were safely in the light of day; for while that would stop the other demons, if Aion was coming, it wouldn't stop him.

Orran carried Sarain for a long while before finally stopping to take a breath. He let her down and together they sat on a large boulder-like rock under the shade of a tree out in the deserted terrain. They sat in silence for a while, collecting their thoughts. Sarain glanced around, and saw no one, human or demon, around for miles. She wondered where they would go, and at first thought of Winston's, but she knew that his place was no longer safe, and a part of her didn't want to return to the scene where she had lost her friend.

Sarain turned to Orran, wondering what he was thinking, she asked, "What do we do now?" He was staring at the sky when he replied, "I know a place, a safe house you could say, that we can hold up in for a while, till things calm down... I kind of kept the knowledge of the place secret from the brotherhood, just in case I ever needed a fallout plan... You know you can't always rely on demons." Hearing this brought a slight smile to Sarain's face, and then Orran added, "I've also got some supplies there: canned food, bottled water, clothes, weapons, and money... There should be enough there to get us out of town." "Wow, you really thought of everything," Sarain stated. Orran turned his gaze to her, and he looked into her eyes as he said, "I needed a backup plan in case I had to get you away from Aion," he then glanced away as he added, "It probably should have been Plan A, but then as you know, Aion is not the easiest man to escape from." Sarain sighed and relayed, "Yeah, I've been running from him for seven years now."

It was a depressing thought, running from a powerful man with countless connections, who was basically immortal. Odds were that they would both die first before Aion would. Sarain glanced at Orran, and by the look on his face, she figured that he was having the same thoughts as her.

Sarain then brought her hand up to her face, and felt the scar of where Kayne had clawed her; there were three total nail marks, and they felt raised up and swollen.

Orran noticed Sarain examining her wound, and he commented, "Don't worry, with the way you heal, it shouldn't scar." But this thought didn't comfort Sarain, instead she replied, "Maybe Kayne was right... Not about me using my looks to get my way with men, but they have certainly caused me some trouble. Maybe it would be better if it scarred, perhaps then I'll stop drawing in people only to get them killed by my lifestyle." "That's crazy, Sarain," Orran told her. She shook her head, saying, "No, it's not."

Sarain eyes then rested on the sword at her side, and she picked it up. Orran gazed at her curiously, and asked, "What are you doing?" But Sarain did not reply, instead she took a hold of her long hair, brought the blade up to it, and sliced through her long locks. She let the hair fall to the ground in a clump, with the remainder hanging down lopsidedly to her chin. Orran gave her an awkward grin as he asked, "Do you feel better now?" "Yes, actually, I do," Sarain stated with a sigh of relief, and she took a deep breath and asked, "So where is this safe house?"

It took Sarain and Orran another couple of hours on foot to finally reach Orran's safe house on the outskirts of town. While it was still technically in the small town of Shaven, the small house sat hidden amongst a heavily wooded area, away from the rest of society; in fact, unless you were looking for the house, you wouldn't even know that it was there.

Sarain gazed around the area, curiously; the environment looked so dramatically different than that of Winston's home, and also that of the brotherhood's headquarters. In truth, the whole town and its surrounding areas varied so much in atmosphere and climate, even though it only stretched for a few miles, that it bordered on miraculous and Sarain wondered if it had anything to do with the heavily supernatural beings that gathered in hidden parts of the small town.

"Well, this is it," Orran stated, as they approached the door, "It's not much, but it's mine." His hand went to the door knob, and then he stopped and turned his attention to Sarain for a second, and said, "Um... There's something else that I haven't told you... I sort of already have some company." Sarain stared at Orran with both curiosity and confusion; she wasn't sure if she could handle any more surprises just yet. "Well... maybe it's better if I just show you, rather than try to explain," Orran said. He then took a hold of the door knob and turned. The door clicked unlocked, and it swung open, they stepped inside, and in a matter of moments, Sarain understood what Orran was trying to tell her.

She saw his guest sprawled out on a couch, with skin so pale it was nearly translucent, and a look in his eyes as though he was barely clinging to life.

Sarain's eyes went wide as she gasped, and said, "Winston!"

Chapter 24

Sarain rushed to Winston's side, initially wanting to hug him, but then stopping short of doing so when she realized how bad of condition he was in. Instead, Sarain took Winston by the hand and gave him a smile that hurt her own face to do so. Winston's usually vibrant blue eyes now looked pale as he stared back at Sarain, looking just as glad to see her as she was seeing him.

"You look like hell," Winston joked in a weak almost whispering tone. "Yeah, because you're the epitome of hotness right now," Sarain muttered with a smile. Winston then weakly raised his hand to the scar on Sarain's face; he gently brushed it with his fingertips, and said, "You'll always be beautiful." Sarain gave him another smile, and then a thought crossed her mind, and the smile suddenly turned to a frown.

"What is it?" Winston asked, looking concerned. "It's about Julianne... Aion killed her," she relayed to him. A sad expression came over Winston's face, and he was silent for a moment, he then looked at Sarain and said, "At least you're alright." "Well, not exactly," Sarain said holding up her hands so that he could see her clawlike nails. Next she pushed back her hair and showed him her pointed ears, "I don't know if it's going to stop," she said. Winston took her hand, and gave it a frail squeeze, "Don't worry about it," he muttered, "It doesn't matter."

Orran watched as the pair interacted, and for once he saw what Winston was so quick to fight for that day he and Sarain had first kissed. The two were clearly more than friends, even if Sarain hadn't realized it herself yet. Though Orran wasn't prepared to step aside, he planned to continue trying to win Sarain back, but he knew now how serious his competition was.

Orran went to the fridge, and retrieved a packet of blood for Winston. As he handed it to the frail and hungry Winston, he pulled Sarain aside. Orran led her back to the kitchen, and then handed her a bottle of water. Sarain thirstily drank it, as Orran began to say, "I hope you're not mad that I didn't tell you about Winston sooner. He was barely hanging on when I found him that I didn't want to say anything until I knew for sure that he was going to make it."

"I get that," Sarain said while wiping away the water that dripped from her mouth, "I just don't understand why you went back to his house to retrieve him." Orran looked at her with surprise and then answered, "I thought it was obvious; I did it for you." This brought a smile to Sarain's face, and she quickly leaned forward and gave Orran a hug. He wrapped his arms around her, and embraced Sarain back. Orran held on to her for a long while, and when he finally let go, he whispered to her, "I have another surprise for you."

Orran then went to a kitchen drawer, and pulled out something that dangled. He held it up so that Sarain could see, and she recognized it immediately, it was her mother's ankh. "I couldn't destroy it. I figured that it was safer here where Kayne couldn't find it," he explained. He then walked over and latched the chain around Sarain's neck. She was so happy to have the pendant back and around her neck once again, that she embraced Orran once more. This time she felt Orran nestle his face up against hers, and Sarain knew that these weren't the actions of a friend, but of a man in love. Sarain held on to Orran a moment longer thinking how after everything that had happened, she wasn't sure anymore how she felt about anyone.

The three of them sat around the dimly lit living room. The room was filled with an awkward sort of silence. Orran broke the silence by saying, "We should run; get out of town, and go as far away from here as we can." Sarain remained silent a minute longer, contemplating what was the best move, and then finally responded, "No, I'm tired of running," then she stared down at her hands and added, "Besides, what kind of life could I have now? It's not like I can just blend in anymore." "Gloves and hoodies can hide that," Orran remarked. "And if these changes don't stop, then what?" Sarain replied, and then added, "I don't want to run; I'm sick of my father having this haunting power over me...No, I want to stay, and fight."

"Us? Against a whole army of demons?" Orran asked sounding very unsure of the idea. "It's not like we haven't done it before," Winston muttered, looking towards Sarain. "I severely doubt you two have ever fought against an Ancient before; all the other demons aside, Aion is the one you should be worried about," Orran explained. "But he wouldn't really kill his own daughter, would he?" Winston remarked. ".....Yes, he would," Sarain stated, "I'm just a failed project to him." Winston gave Sarain a look of concern, but then said, "Well, either way, if you want to fight, I'll fight with you."

Sarain then looked to Orran, awaiting his decision. He let out a sigh of disappointment, but answered, "I go wherever you go." "Good," Sarain stated, "As soon as we're all feeling well enough, training will begin."

Over the next few days, Sarain and Winston, both, spent their time sleeping and eating. The weakness and exhaustion from the previous days had taken its toll on Sarain, and she felt as though she had slipped into a hibernating state. Her thoughts and dreams had become a blur as well as the days and nights, since the house was kept dark for Winston, whom was also struggling to regain his strength and energy.

Meanwhile, Orran hovered about keeping a watchful eye on both his guests; getting them food or drink whenever they required it, and sketching out tactical strategy ideas in his free time. He cleaned and prepared weapons for battle, mostly blades since bullets often bounced off the demons shell like skin, and explosives would be too dangerous in such small quarters as the cave tunnels.

Both Orran and Winston slept in the living room; Winston on the couch, and Orran on a mat on the floor. Sarain had the bedroom to herself, where she tossed and turned in her sleep. Though she had trouble remembering her dreams, she knew that they were violent; likely in view of the fact that she had quite a battle in her near future.

Finally, one day Sarain woke up around dusk feeling more rejuvenated than she had in a long while. She opened up the bedroom door to see Winston sitting up on the couch, drinking a blood packet, with more coloring to his skin than he had had when she showed up. Given he was still a pale man, but now he looked normal enough for a vil sang.

"Feeling better?" Winston asked her. "I feel well enough," Sarain stated, and then asked, "Are you up for training?" Winston slowly got up from his spot on the couch, and replied, "I'll have to take it slow, but I think I can manage." Sarain then peered around the room and commented, "Where's Orran?" "I think he went out while we were asleep. I'm sure he'll be back soon... He never seems to leave your side for long," Winston replied, and then added, "No wonder you've been hung up on the guy all these years, he is quite the hero; even saved my sorry hide."

Sarain glanced at Winston, once she realized that he was being serious and not sarcastic, and said, "It's not like you haven't been my hero a time or two." Winston gave her a smile, and then responded, "Well you're a stubborn woman, you probably would have found some way to save yourself, if I hadn't have come along." "Maybe…" Sarain remarked sounding lost in thought, and then she said something that caught Winston by surprise; "Do you ever wonder what would have happened if I hadn't left back then?" Without having to give the question thought, Winston replied, "All the time." "…..Ya…Well, so do I," Sarain muttered. Winston then took a few steps towards her as he said, "I wish I could have been there for you when you found out about your father, and started going through the changes. I know it's not an easy thing to deal with." Winston then extended his hand, and he went to take Sarain's. His fingertips brushed against her palm, and he noticed that her skin was cold like his.

Suddenly the front door creaked open, and Sarain quickly pulled her hand back and away from Winston's. Orran stepped in carrying brown paper bags full of supplies, and Winston stepped away from Sarain, knowing that he would no longer have her undivided attention. But for a moment, he had felt like the center of her world, and he could have sworn he saw a look in Sarain's eyes that he hadn't seen since the night they made love so many years ago. A look as though she needed him.

Chapter 25

Orran unloaded food for all of them, though he looked to Winston when he said, "Blood packets are getting harder to get a hold of now that I have the brotherhood looking for me. There is a lot of wildlife here in the area; I think we'll have to start catching your meals." Orran next looked to Sarain, and stated, "I got fresh milk and eggs to help get your strength up, though you look well enough to maybe start some training today." "Ya, I am feeling better," Sarain remarked. "Well the sun is pretty much down, so we can all go outside for some light training, if you'd like," he replied. Sarain nodded her head in agreement.

After Orran finished putting away the supplies, they all stepped outside into the cool early evening air. Winston took a deep breath and then exhaled, seeming glad to finally be out in the night air once again. Sarain looked up to the sky, seeing the stars barely beginning to emerge, then glanced to the men by her side; Orran and Winston were chatting on about the surrounding woods, and Sarain was surprised to see smiles on both men's faces. She never thought that she would one day spend time with both the men who had made a strong presence in her life, and with everything out in the open.

"What should we do first?" Sarain spoke, getting the men's attention. Orran looked to Sarain and then glanced towards the door where three swords where laying on the ground, and said, "If you feel ready for it." Sarain walked over and picked up a blade, and then preceded to hand the other two to Winston and Orran.

They spread out into a triangular form, preparing to spar with one another. "Keep it clean," Sarain announced, hoping that Winston and Orran's newfound bond stayed intact. They all exchanged glances, waiting to see who would be the first to strike. Sarain was the first to move, she charged Orran, who immediately dodged her attack. She swung her blade again, and this time it was Winston who blocked her blade with his own. Protecting Orran, Winston swung at Sarain, it wasn't a great swing, in fact it was rather slow, and Sarain thought she noticed Winston trying to catch his breath. Suddenly, Sarain's focus was broken when she realized Orran was sneaking up on her; he and Winston had worked as a team to catch her off guard. She turned just in time to see Orran tackle her, and she went tumbling to the ground, her blade slipping from her grasp.

Orran stared down at Sarain, still on top of her, as he stated, "That was too easy; you need to keep better attention to your surroundings. If I had been a demon, I would be eating you right now." Orran waited for Sarain to make a witty remark, but instead he noticed her cheeks turning red, and wasn't sure if it was because she had made such a blatant fighting mistake, or because he was still on top of her. Orran then quickly stood up and extended a hand to pull Sarain to her feet. After she was up off the ground, her hand lingered inside his for a moment before Sarain finally let go. She gave a swift glance to Winston who had been watching the whole time. He looked away and then muttered, "You know, perhaps I'm still not ready for sparring. I think I'll try my hand at catching some of the wildlife around here that you spoke of."

Winston dropped down his blade, saying, "I don't need this to hunt," and then walked off into the woods, with his head hanging with melancholy. Sarain knew that he had left because he was feeling like a third wheel; still she was surprised that Winston would willingly leave her alone with Orran. Perhaps he felt he owed Orran for saving his life, or perhaps he truly thought that Sarain was better off with him; either way, Sarain now stood alone and in awkward silence with her old friend.

"Did you want to continue to train?" Orran asked, finally breaking the silence. Sarain shook her head, and then went to sit on the stoop at the house's front door. Orran put down his sword, and then sat next to Sarain. Her hand was resting on her thigh, and after a moment of yet another silence, Orran began to reach out for her hand with his. The palm of his hand rested on top of hers, and his skin felt so much warmer than her own. Sarain sighed, and quickly stood up.

Orran gazed up at her with surprise, and asked, "What's wrong?" "It's just... there's something that's been bugging me for awhile," she replied. "Well, what is it?" he inquired. Sarain looked to Orran with a moment of hesitation before finally working up the nerve to ask, "How did you even get started with Aion? When did he get to you?" Orran sighed and turned to her as he explained, "It was right after the massacre, after the other demons had fled, and I guess you had as well... I felt the warmth of the sun against my skin, and I opened up my eyes to see that dawn had finally come. And then I saw this man staring down at me, and he looked at me with the same eyes as yours, and I thought I had been saved... He told me that I was going to die, and then he said that he would save me if I promised to help him one day, if he ever decided to call upon me... I didn't want to die... So I said yes, and then he slit his wrist and fed me his blood, and then the next thing I know, I'm waking up again to some hunters stumbling upon our camp, and looking for survivors. They looked at my wounds and said that though they looked bad, I seemed strong and that I was going to be fine."

"So he just left you?" Sarain asked with confusion. "Yes, but only for awhile... Nothing had changed; I still felt the same; no weakness to sunlight, no thirst for blood. So I thought that I had dreamt the whole thing, and then I started to notice that things were getting easier, hunting especially. I was getting stronger without having to try. And then one day he showed up, asking for my help," Orran relayed, "You have to understand, I owed him my life. And at first he only asked me to help him with simple things... and then he had me help him identify hunters. At first he claimed it was so that he could avoid them, and then they started disappearing. I figured out what he was doing, and I told him that I wanted nothing more to do with him." "So then why did you stay?" Sarain questioned, puzzled. Orran then looked away, a bit unsure if he should answer, before saying, "Because he told me that he knew where you were, and that if I ever wanted to see you again, I needed to do everything he said... Years went by, and Aion kept saying that I wasn't ready to see you yet; that I needed to be sculpted and prepared into someone worthy of you... Finally, here recently, he came to me saying that I was ready to see you again. He wanted me to connect with you and then bring you into the brotherhood."

Sarain forced out a sarcastic laugh before remarking, "I guess we really wrecked that plan." Orran smirked, and then said seriously, "Aion hadn't anticipated Winston's loyalty to you... When he learned of your connection with a vil sang; he didn't consider him as a threat, but as more of a nuisance. He figured, if worse came to worst, he could bring Winston into the brotherhood as well... But then, you know what happened with that; Winston couldn't be persuaded over."

Sarain was quiet again; the mere mention of Winston's name was almost like having him there for the conversation. She now felt guilty for wrecking both men's lives, and to get her mind off that subject, she decided to ask Orran another question she had been wondering about him. "Have you been having the seizures?" Orran stared at her with puzzlement for a moment, and then asked, "Like the one you had after

Aion fed you that girl's blood?" "Yes, sort of like that," Sarain replied. Orran gave her a worried look as he answered, "No." Sarain sighed, both glad and disappointed. "Then I guess it's just me," she announced, and observed, "You don't seem to be having the demonic changes that I've been going through, but then my father's blood is stronger in me."

Sarain went to look away, but Orran stopped her, by saying, "I don't care that you're different. Hell, I don't even notice it! I look at you, and all I see is the same beautiful girl that I have always known. The same girl that I have always protected, and will always protect. You could grow ten feet tall, and have stone skin, and I'd still be willing to die for you."

Orran stood up, and approached Sarain. "I've loved you since we were kids," he told her, "I could never let a little thing like you becoming a demon, change that." Sarain gave him a teary smile, and then Orran began to lean in. Her lips started to quiver as she saw his face growing closer. His warm breath beat against her skin, and she felt her cheeks turning red again. Tension built up in her body, and she became more and more nervous. Orran's bottom lip brushed up against Sarain's, and a kiss seemed inevitable. But before their lips could meet, Sarain found herself pulling away at the sound of leaves crunching.

She stepped away from Orran just in time to see Winston approaching with a rabbit in hand. "It looks like I was quick enough to catch this guy," Winston announced holding up the rabbit like a trophy. Then he glanced at Orran and Sarain, and asked, "What? What did I miss?"

Chapter 26

Over the next few days, the three of them continued to train and grow stronger. Sarain didn't find herself alone with either man, but instead they pretty much did everything as a group. When they weren't sparring, they told stories of their youth; Sarain and Orran spoke of life in their clan, and Winston told them of growing up in an older and much less modern time. The three of them bonded as friends, and for once in a long time for all of them, it was like having a family.

The rapidly approaching day of battle had arrived, and the three of them went over their plan of attack. They doubted that Aion would expect for them to come back and attack the brotherhood after everything that had happened. Likely they would have assumed that Orran and Sarain had fled and that Winston was dead. The plan was for Orran to wire the entrance only with explosives just before dusk. When the bomb went off it would cause the demons inside to become alert and then try to flee through what remained of the entrance, which should only allow a few if not one demon at a time to get through. This is where the rest of them stepped in. At dusk, as the demons began to flee, they planned to step in with blades in hand, and strike down each demon that emerged. The hope was that eventually Kayne and Aion would emerge, and that the three of them would take them out together. It wasn't an elaborate plan, but it was the best that they could manage with the lack of an army.

They suited up with as many blades as they could carry: swords, daggers, and machetes strapped to their bodies. Then with Winston cloaked under thick and heavy fabric, they set off to head near the brotherhood's cavern. They trekked the rocky terrain up the mountainside with barely a word; there was something ominous about this trip, like they knew that they weren't all going to be making the trip back. Once they were in close distance, Sarain and Winston lay and waited in the shadows as Orran left to prepare the explosives. It took him longer than they had anticipated, and by the time Orran returned to them it was already dusk, and they just hoped that the demons inside hadn't gone to go out towards the entrance.

The three of them crouched in position behind a large boulder to protect them from the blast, and covered their ears as Orran set off the explosives. A loud, almost deafening, blast went off; dust and dirt filled the air with a reddish brown haze, as pebble sized rubble fell from the sky. The dust started to settle, and for a while everything was quiet, and then a low rumble began. The ground started the shake, and at first Sarain thought that the ground was going to cave in, until she realized that the tremors weren't a result of the explosion, but instead a result of it alerting the demons within the mountain: the tremors were from all the beasts within, suddenly getting up and rushing towards the exit. The demon army had to be much vaster than Sarain had anticipated.

They readied themselves, as they heard digging from inside the cavern. Each had a sword in hand, and they exchanged glances as they waited for the first demon to break through. Finally a clawed hand poked out from behind the rubble, and a demon emerged, soon followed by another, and then another. They raced towards the beasts, slashing away at their thick skin. Demons began coming quickly, and the trio worked hard to keep their numbers down.

Sarain glanced over to see Orran chopping beasts one by one with incredible speed, and then checked to see Winston who was fighting further away, and on the outskirts of the battle. She thrust her blade through another monster, and moved on to the next just as she heard a grumble coming from the sky. Droplets of rain fell onto her skin, and soon a light drizzle turned into a heavy downpour. The ground became soft and muddy, and Sarain started having to watch her footing with the cliffs and numerous demons near. She watched as more beasts scattered and slipped out from the cave's demolished entrance.

Winston struggled to up his speed, but still felt as though his stomach muscles hadn't completely rejuvenated since being run through. Suddenly a thick and heavy looking demon caught his eye; the beast was large and looked as though it had a shell on its back. Winston swung his sword at the creature, and the demon surprisingly twisted sideways so much so that its body contorted so that its shell moved almost completely to its front, taking the brunt of Winston's hit. The impact made a loud clang, and Winston noticed a crack forming midway and across the blade of his sword. He swung again, and this time the sword broke in half. The beast began to charge Winston, who quickly threw down the busted blade and detached a machete strapped to his side. He thrust the short sword forward, just in time to have the beast run on to it, impaling itself on the blade. Winston used his foot to kick and force the creature off, and the demon dropped and rolled off the side of the cliff, dead.

Orran slashed and decapitated another monster, then quickly turned with his long wet hair whipping around with him, and stabbed at a different beast. He caught a glimpse of Sarain fighting, she appeared to have gotten her strength back as she ran up a demon's backside, and stabbed her sword downward and through its head.

The fighting continued on for hours. The rain began to let up, and then eventually stopped altogether. The demons' numbers started to dwindle, but there was still no sign of either Kayne or Aion. Winston had moved deeper into the battle, and Sarain and Orran stood on either side of the cave opening, with Sarain close to the edge of a cliff. It looked as though the battle was dying down, and Sarain wondered how many demons could really be left. And then just like that, the beasts stopped coming out of the cave. The three of them killed the rest of the monsters that remained, and then exchanged glances as they began to approach one another.

"That can't be it," said a tired Winston, "that was way too easy." "I haven't seen Kayne nor Aion, and I severely doubt they snuck past us," a frustrated Orran stated. "I didn't see them either," Sarain remarked. They all sighed, and took in deep breaths as though this was the first opportunity to do so, and then they all began to wonder what was to come next.

Suddenly the group of them all heard what sounded like a horn blowing from somewhere in the cavern, and soon after, a horde of demons came busting out the cave at once; breaking through the stone, and destroying what little form of the cave there was left. The demons rushed the group, as they all began to raise their blades once again. They slashed wildly at the numerous beasts, clawed limbs and black blood flew through the air. Sarain pulled her sword out of the stomach of a demon, and then looked up just in time to see Kayne emerge out of the wrecked tunnel.

He stood tall and looming, and still had only a stump where one of his wings had once been. Sarain made motion to move toward him, tightening the grip on her sword in hand. Kayne merely watched as Sarain approached him, and then she saw him raise up one of his arms with something dark in his hand.

Suddenly a loud crack echoed through the night. Both Winston and Orran turned in mid battle to see what had caused the deafening noise, but Sarain had realized immediately when she felt the bullet go through her shoulder. Orran saw the gun in Kayne's hand, and abruptly began slicing his way through the horde of

beasts to get to him. Winston saw Sarain fall backwards
onto the ground, and rushed to get to her side. He pushed
his way past demons, and just as he was about a yard
away, he suddenly felt the intense pain of a blade slicing
through him. Winston gazed down to see the hilt of the
sword he had broken earlier, sticking out of his stomach.
A small demon had apparently picked up the blade, and
used it like a dagger; Winston hadn't even seen the
creature sneak up next to him. He staggered for a
moment, and then fell to his knees. And as he collapsed
forward, he realized that the wounded Sarain was still just
out of his reach.

Kayne squeezed out another shot, and the bullet
hit the ground near Sarain's head. Kayne struggled to line
up a decent shot with his large clawed hands and his
depth perception skewed by the fact that he was missing
an eye. Sarain tried to get up to move away, and in doing
so she caught a glimpse of Orran struggling to get his
sword out of the stone like exterior of a beast that he had
just impaled. He watched as Kayne aimed his gun once
again at Sarain, and decided to abandon his sword. Orran
ran towards the monstrous beast, and as he neared, Kayne
suddenly sensed his presence, despite the fact that Orran
was racing toward him on the side of his missing eye.
Kayne turned toward the man and fired the gun, and a
bullet shot out and hit Orran square in the chest.

Sarain gasped as she saw Orran take the hit, but to
her shock, this did not stop him. He continued to run
toward Kayne, and for a second his eyes met with
Sarain's, and it was then when she realized what he had
decided to do when he abandoned his sword.

Sarain shouted, "No," as she watched Orran slam into Kayne, tackling him hard. He threw all his weight and strength up against the beast, causing Kayne to stumble back. Orran continued to press despite Kayne pushing him with all his might, until they neared the cliff's edge, but still Orran's feet did not stop. He shoved Kayne over the edge, with the beast grabbing onto him, and digging his claws deep into Orran's back. The two of them went off the cliff, while Sarain screamed so loudly that she didn't hear the sickening crash as they hit the bottom.

Sarain strained to get up, with pain shooting through her arm and shoulder, as she pushed herself up into a stand. She staggered towards the cliff's edge, and then slowly peered down. Her vision blurred at the sight of black and red blood, scattered on the rocks below, and Sarain realized that she was crying. She dropped to her knees with tears flooding out her eyes, and sobbed so hard, that she wasn't sure if she would ever stop.

Soon she felt a hand on her good shoulder, and gazed up to see Winston standing next to her, staring down at her with concern. She was so glad to see him that she hugged onto his leg, not even noticing the bloody wound at his stomach, or the small demon that laid dead a few feet away from them that had tried to sneak up on Sarain, but now had a broken sword sticking out of its face.

Sarain continued to sob a moment longer, until finally wiping her eyes and lifting her head to peer around and see how many demons were left. It looked as though the few that had remained had dispersed and ran off. The rest of the army was dead; their bodies littering the surface of the mountain, with some of the carcasses having been thrown off the cliff so that others could move through.

Suddenly the sound of rustling caught Sarain's attention, and her eyes went to the collapsed cave's entrance. She noticed that the pebbles and rocks were shaking, and then with a flash of light she saw her father standing there, having teleported out of the cave.

Their violet eyes met in that moment, and Sarain heard herself mutter the word, "You!" Aion scanned the damage that covered the ground around them, his army had been defeated, but when he looked to Sarain, a smile formed on his face, and then another flash of light engulfed him, and just as quickly, he was gone.

Chapter 27

It was a bright and beautiful day; the sun shined brilliantly with only a few white puffy clouds up in the sky. Two teenagers joked happily; glad to have the day off from training while the clan elders did trading with some local merchants and hunters in the area. They sat around at a small park next to where the adults had gone to do business.

The boy, who was the older of the two, proceeded to mess up the girl's hair, saying, "There! Now you look perfect for everyday society!" She gazed at him, annoyed, and asked, "Why'd you have to do that?" "Why'd you have to put on makeup? You look silly!" the boy remarked, "What, are you expecting to meet someone? You got a hot date?" She shot him an angry look, and then said, "Stop being stupid!" "You're the one being stupid, you look better without that junk on your face," he replied. "Since when do you look?" she shot back. The boy then grabbed the girl by the hand and stated, "I've been looking for a while now." She blushed, and then stared up into the boy's hazel eyes, as she muttered soft and bashfully, "Orran."

A woman suddenly broke the tension building between the two teenagers, as she approached them with a camera in hand saying, "Would you guys like for me to take your picture? It's only two dollars." Orran turned toward the woman and smiled, answering, "Sure!" And then he left go of the girl's hand, and wrapped his arm around her shoulders. The two of them stared into the lens, and in moments, the flash went off, lighting up the girl's unique violet eyes.

After a minute the woman handed the teenagers a Polaroid. Orran looked at it first and then handed it to the girl, saying, "Here, Sarain, I want you to have this." "What makes you think I want it?" she teased. He smiled at her as he replied, "Because I've seen you looking at me too." Sarain blushed again, and then took the photo from her friend, with a nervous smile on her face.

A moment later, they saw the clan's chief, Delmar, and a few other clan elders, approaching with supplies in hand. Orran quickly moved to help carry the provisions, and Sarain immediately hid the picture in her pocket. A frown began to form on her face, as she realized that she wasn't sure when she'd get another unsupervised moment with Orran. She just hoped that it would be soon.

"Oh god, he's getting away," Sarain shouted, "We have to go after him!" Winston quickly extended his hand down to Sarain, and as she took a hold of it, so that he could help her up, she noticed how her clawed fingers, interweaving with his, looked so much more demonic than his own. Between the two, Winston was the one who appeared more human.

Sarain stood up and looked around, trying to figure out where Aion could have gone, and how far his teleporting could have taken him. She scanned the rocky landscape and then her eyes stopped when she saw a glint of light flash up high on the mountaintop. "Why would he be going up there?" she wondered, but didn't want to waste the time to figure out. "We have to hurry," she shouted, "Before he gets away!" But Winston didn't budge, instead he asked, "If he can teleport like that, what makes you think he won't just continue to run? Why stop and fight with us, and in that case, why make us chase him at all?"

Sarain stared at Winston, perplexedly for a moment, and then said, "I know my father; he isn't going to just run away like a coward. He's waiting up there to fight with me… He just wants to make me work for it." "Ok, that's all I needed to hear. Let's go," Winston stated and then moved to start climbing the rocky mountain side. Sarain watched as Winston strained to lift his leg, and then finally noticed the bloody wound at his side.

Suddenly a revelation came to Sarain that she may not make it out of this battle alive, and she realized that she didn't want Winston to die for her cause. She had lost too many people over the years, and even knowing that her own life was at serious risk, for some reason it was the idea of Winston dying as well that was more than she could handle.

Sarain looked up towards the sky, the stars had already begun to fade, and the night sky looked more blue than black. She knew that the dawn wasn't too long off. Sarain took a deep breath to prepare her for what she was about to say next; "Winston, you're not coming."

Winston stopped trying to climb the side, he dropped back down about a foot, and then stared at Sarain with confusion, "You don't want me to go?" he asked, and then took a deep breath before saying, "I'm not going to let you fight Aion alone." Sarain sighed, and then stated, "You're hurt; you're only going to slow me down." "I'm fine," he insisted looking frustrated with her. "It's almost dawn," she pressed, hoping to get her point across to him. "I can still be of use," Winston argued. "You're weak and you're just going to get in my way!" she hollered. And then suddenly he yelled, "I love you too much to let you go!"

"I don't love you!" Sarain shouted with pain hitting her heart. "You don't mean that!" Winston cried out, as tears began rolling down his face. His chest shook with a heavy and unsteady breath.

A tear escaped Sarain's eye as she said, "I've never loved you," her voice was weak, and her words trembled. Winston gasped and stood there staring at her blankly. Sarain mustered her strength, and spoke as firmly as she could, saying, "Leave."

"No," Winston stated with a solemn expression. Sarain clenched her teeth, took a deep breath, and repeated stronger than before, "Leave!"

A look of anger came over Winston's face as he stared into Sarain's eyes, silently. He began to move to walk away, but then stopped short. He turned back around and quickly moved toward her. He grabbed her by her good arm and pulled her to him. With his other hand, he grabbed the back of Sarain's head, his fingers entwining through her hair, and he forced his lips against Sarain's, pressing them firmly against hers. She felt his lips part, and then kiss her again. His lips were damp and salty with his tears, and for the first time his skin actually warmed Sarain's.

Sarain began to feel herself almost kissing Winston back, when she realized what she was about to do, and stopped herself. Sarain's heart begged her to hold on to Winston, and she longed to kiss him back. But she reluctantly pushed Winston away, and quickly slapped him across the face to mask her own feelings for him. She went to turn away when she felt that her hand was still lingering on Winston's cheek. Tears ran down Sarain's face as she gazed up at him to see him staring down at her with pain in his eyes. And it was that moment that Winston finally saw what Sarain was trying so hard to hide from him. They didn't say anything for a while, not until Sarain managed to mutter softly, "Just go," and Winston complied.

He watched her walk away, knowing that it was likely the last time he was ever going to see her, and then he whispered into the wind, "I love you, too."

Chapter 28

Winston waited there, among the slaughtered demons, for a few minutes longer, hoping that Sarain might change her mind, turn around, and come back to him. But she was already long out of sight. He then looked to the sky, seeing it turning bluer by the minute, and realized the time had come for him to leave to take shelter.

He turned to begin heading back to the mess that was his home, when he saw a man standing there, so unnaturally quiet, waiting to catch Winston's attention. "How long have you been standing there?" Winston muttered without fear. "Only a few seconds," Aion replied. "So I guess it was your plan all along to separate us," Winston remarked. Aion smiled, a sly grin, and stated, "I knew my daughter wouldn't allow you to give your life up for hers; she's so predictable in that way." "...So then is this the point where you take matters into your own hands, and kill me?" Winston asked, ready to face the worst.

Aion slowly started to approach Winston, while slipping a dagger out from his sleeve. "Is that really all you think it takes to kill me?" Winston questioned, but didn't get an answer from Aion, once again. Aion then stopped in front of him, and began to raise the dagger up into the air. He stopped at about throat level, and Winston rolled his eyes at the fact that Aion was dragging things out, like he wanted him to beg for his life, but Winston refused to give Aion that pleasure. Instead, he waited for the inevitable stabbing, but in a moment found himself in shock, as he witness Aion suddenly raise and slash his own wrist. And then in a blink of an eye, Aion was behind him with his arm wrapped around his own, to hold him back, and his wrist pressed against his lips. Aion's thick blood gushed into Winston mouth, and he choked in astonishment.

The blood tasted different and strange to Winston, and as he gagged once more on the thickness and speed that the blood flowed into his mouth, he suddenly felt himself falling to his knees. He soon realized that Aion had vanished, and left him alone. Winston started to feel sick as he looked up at the sky seeing it getting ever bluer, and realized that he had no time to think over what had just happened. He needed to get down off this mountain quickly before the day came.

Sarain trekked up the deserted mountainside, wondering if Aion would truly be just simply waiting for her at the top of the mountain. Sarain thought about all the reasons why she hated her father; she thought of the attack on her clan, her having to grow up alone, she thought of Eddie, and then Orran; and knew that everything bad that had ever happened to her was in some way linked to Aion. And not only had he ruined her life, as well as Orran's, but he had also ruined the life of her mother, Ariana. He had left her mother with child and with a father so angry at her that he would one day poison her to death. So many lives would have been saved if Aion and Ariana had never met. Sarain thought of how if she didn't exist, so many others would still be here living their lives. Sarain knew she had saved many lives over the years, but wondered how many others could have been saved if her clan of hunters had survived. She was prepared to do anything to stop her father, even if it meant that she would not be walking back down this mountain, and even if it meant that she would never see Winston again.

Sarain felt her hatred for Aion growing deep inside her, believing that she needed this anger to fuel her, and give her the strength to defeat him. She felt her eyes begin to glow, her fangs begin to descend, and then her blood begin to boil. Then she surprisingly felt her head begin to grow hotter and hotter than it should. Suddenly a sharp searing pain pulsated in her brain and then throughout her body. She felt her body seize as she dropped to her knees, clutching her head, but soon it wasn't her head that hurt, but instead her chest. It burned as though on fire, and Sarain found herself tearing at all that clung to her. Then just as quickly, the pain stopped, and as Sarain stared down, she realized why.

She gazed upon the ground to see her mother's ankh lying there, having been torn off in her painful and infuriated state. The pendant had burned her, and in fact had left a scorched mark upon her skin. Sarain felt her heart sink as she realized that her demonic changes were still continuing to occur. She stared down at the ankh for a moment longer, and she knew that she had to leave it behind. Sarain reluctantly stood up, and then continued on with her trek.

It wasn't long after that Sarain found herself at the end of her journey. She walked up onto the clearing that lay at the top of the mountain. The sky was turning blue, and the stars were now completely gone. A gentle breeze blew and Sarain appeared to be alone. She stared down at the landscape below; stone and trees so far down, and everything seemed so small. She stood in the center of the clearing, took a deep breath, and said, "I knew that you would be waiting here for me."

"I knew that you would come alone," Aion said from behind her. She sighed, and then turned around to face her father, and asked with a heavy heart, "Why all this? Why everything?... Why Orran?" "That's a lot of questions," Aion remarked, he then gazed at his daughter with no emotion on his face, and began to say, "The night my army attacked your clan, my general, Sephor, came back to me talking of a violet eyed girl with incredible power; he suspected that you were my daughter. Afterwards when I went looking for you, I found a boy barely clinging to life, and when this boy stared up into my eyes he spoke with love for this violet eyed girl. It was then that I knew that one day this boy might prove to be useful."

Sarain stared up at her father with tears in her eyes, struggling to keep her composure as she said, "Fine, but why kill my entire clan and not just Delmar?"

"Because they all followed your grandfather blindly, and they all failed to save your mother from him," Aion answered, and that's when Sarain noticed a slip in her father's stature. He had winced when speaking of her mother. A realization suddenly came to her, and Sarain felt as though everything now made sense; "You're still in love with her; that's what this has all been about," Sarain spoke in amazement.

Aion stared at his daughter, but did not say a word. She felt astonished, saying, "That's why you've been trying so hard to get me to join you. It had nothing to do with me leading your army, you just wanted the last piece of Ariana by your side!"

Sarain saw a tear run down her father's face at the mention of her mother's name, and it was in that moment, that her hatred for her father began to fade away. She looked upon her father with new eyes, and now all she could feel for him was pity.

The sun began to rise on a new and beautiful day, and Sarain knew what it was that she had to do to put a stop to all their suffering. She let the sword in her hand fall to the ground, and she took a step towards her father. She felt her skin warming as she wrapped her arms around Aion, and he sobbed while holding on to his daughter, not caring that her skin was beginning to burn his.

Sarain then closed her eyes and let the sun engulf her. In her mind, she saw her mother smiling, and with a final notion she thought of how warmly embracing the sun was, and it was nice.

Epilogue

The following night, Winston made the long trek back up the mountainside, hoping to find some evidence of the outcome of the fight, and what had happened to Sarain. His heart felt heavy the whole trip up, but the wound he had received to his side the night before had already healed; even faster than he was used to.

The night was peacefully quiet, and all the demons' bodies left from the night before had burnt up with the day, and no evidence of the grizzly battle remained. Winston neared the top of the mountain, expecting that that was where he would find the answer he sought, but it was there at his feet that he realized what had happened. The light of the moon gleamed off the shiny piece of metal that lay on the ground. Winston stopped and bent down to examine the object. Tears fell from his eyes as he picked it up, and let it burn against his skin.

Winston held onto Sarain's ankh pendant, and he knew that there was no point in looking any further; he would not find her body. He sobbed knowing that his love was gone, and in his anguish, he felt something stir from deep within him.

He felt the painful fury rise up inside of him and burn throughout his body. His eyes blazed fiercely in his skull, and he felt his sorrow turn to extreme pain. Winston's body began to convulse, and he felt something that he hadn't felt since the day he was first made; he felt his body growing stronger, and then he realized that the ankh no longer burned his flesh.

Everything was dark and cold around her, and it wasn't until she heard a soft voice saying, "Wake up, my child," that she finally opened up her perfectly ordinary brown eyes, and looked upon her new world.

End of Book 3

Finish Sarain's adventure in Vile Blood 4: Rebirth
available in ebook and soon to be in print!

Thanks for reading!

Jen Golembiewski